GOING BACK

Jane and E   dley-
cott, a hous   len —
a house that   years
of the Secon

It was al   the
children; for   from
time to time, for Jane and Edward's tyrannical and
much feared father; and home for Mike, the conscientious objector or 'conchie' and adored friend of the
children.

It is a place that houses many memories for Jane and
we return to Medleycott with her, now grown up and
with children of her own. Past and present merge into
one and the years fuse together as the memories come
flooding back . . .

A beautiful and evocative novel by this ever-popular
children's author.

Penelope Lively was born in Egypt. She read history
at St Anne's College, Oxford, married a don and has
two children. She lives in a sixteenth-century farmhouse, where she has written several very distinguished
novels for adults and children, one of which, *Moon
Tiger*, won the Booker Prize.

Other books by Penelope Lively

The Driftway
Fanny and the Monsters
The Ghost of Thomas Kempe
The House in Norham Gardens
The Revenge of Samuel Stokes
A Stitch in Time
Uninvited Ghosts
The Wild Hunt of Hagworthy

PENELOPE LIVELY

Going Back

PUFFIN BOOKS

PUFFIN BOOKS

Published by the Penguin Group
27 Wrights Lane, London w8 5tz, England
Viking Penguin Inc., 40 West 23rd Street, New York, New York 10010, USA
Penguin Books Australia Ltd, Ringwood, Victoria, Australia
Penguin Books Canada Ltd, 2801 John Street, Markham, Ontario, Canada l3r 1b4
Penguin Books (NZ) Ltd, 182–190 Wairau Road, Auckland 10, New Zealand

Penguin Books Ltd, Registered Offices: Harmondsworth, Middlesex, England

First published by William Heinemann Ltd 1975
Published in Puffin Books 1986
3 5 7 9 10 8 6 4

Made and printed in Great Britain by
Richard Clay Ltd, Bungay, Suffolk
Typeset in Garamond

To Vanessa and John

———————————————————————————

It seems smaller, going back: the garden, the house, everything. But the garden, especially. When I was a small child it was infinite: lawns, paths, high hedges, the rose garden, the long reach of the kitchen garden, the spinney with the silver birches. It was a completed world; beyond lay nothingness. Space. Limbo.

In fact, I now see, a landscape of fields and hills and lanes, tranquil and harmless—but then it was the un-predictable, into which one did not go. We turned back at the gates. The five-barred stable gate, the white gate by the tennis lawn, the drive gates. These defined our world: the safe, controlled world of the garden.

Today, coming out of the other, unpredictable world, it was the garden that was somehow strange—a planned and ordered place amid the random fields and trees.

We stopped the car outside the drive gates.

'I won't be long,' I said.

My husband opened a newspaper. 'No need to hurry.'

I walked down the drive. The leaves were falling, lying in glowing piles at either side. And the conkers. It was a good conker year, I could see. Years ago, years and years ago, when we were five and six, Edward and I, even the drive was a daring extension of our world. We lived then in the hedged bit beyond the kitchen, where the swing was. And then as we got older we made sorties up here, for the conkers and the wild strawberries, and down to the stables, and to the ha-ha at the bottom of the big lawn, and across the field to the spinney and the stream. And then somehow we were over the gates and out there, in that undefined world of light and shape and shadow, and there were no surprises out there any more. No lions; no dragons.

Only the bull in Mr Pitt's field, down at Rodhuish. And daft Ted in the village. And a rabbit's head in the old quarry.

Remembering is like that. There's what you remember, and then there are the things that have never stopped happening, because they are there always, in your head. We are at the orchid place in the quarry, Edward and I, and a rabbit's head lies among the purple-spotted orchids, where the bees unconcernedly feed, a dreadful, shameful thing, and we turn tail and run ... We sit by the canal in the iris garden, and Edward mangles daisies, his fingers yellow-stained ... I am standing in a farmyard, and an aeroplane creeps along the sky above a barn ... There is a noise of rooks, and a grey-haired woman puts her hand on my shoulder in a quiet room where a clock ticks.

The rooks were loud today. I turned off the drive and went through the gate into the kitchen garden, and stood listening to them, and smelling bonfire smoke. It seems, now, the noise of Medleycott: hearing them, elsewhere, I am back there, always. And yet I don't remember them when I was a small child; it was the pigeons, then, the pigeons rumbling on the roof. Only later, when I was twelve, and fourteen, and sixteen, when Edward was at school, do I remember rooks.

I walked up the grass path to the top of the kitchen garden, where the plums used to be, the old Victorias, but they had gone. Worn out, I suppose, and cut down. The kitchen garden slopes away to the high macrocarpa hedge at the bottom, beyond which is the garden proper, and the house, just visible with pigeons walking about on the roof. Looking down it, I saw that everything was green with weed. Groundsel and couch grass and ground elder, and long trails of bindweed spiralling up the cordon apples and the gooseberry bushes. The place where the lilies of the valley used to be was choked with young thistles, and the cucumber frames were all cracked and rotten. I tried to open one but it broke in my hands, and there were only weeds inside. He must have given up the kitchen garden, father, before he died. There was thyme, though, big bushes of it doing well down by the quince tree. I pinched it, to smell.

I walked past the rubbish heap and the potting-shed. That was a place we used to avoid. There was a gardener once—not Sandy—who used to trap moles and nail the carcasses to the potting-shed door. We came upon them once unawares, the shrivelled little corpses, crucified there in that dark corner, and we stood transfixed with horror before we ran away, not looking at each other, back to some other part of the garden. We never went there again but always, tacitly, made a wide circuit to avoid the place. Years later, I still kept away, forgetting why, by then. Now, I looked into the potting-shed and

3

saw a rusting mower, garden tools, pink with Somerset earth, hanks of raffia hanging from hooks, cobwebbed columns of flower-pots. No moles.

We caught a mole once, Edward and I. That would be when we were about ten and eleven, I suppose, towards the end of the war. We were watering our garden—the place by the greenhouse where we grew lettuces and radishes and spring onions—and all of a sudden the earth heaved and shook and from out between two lettuces there burst a mole, all wriggling black fur and pink spade-hands. It dashed off down the path, squeaking, I remember. That was what most enthralled us: we hadn't realized moles squeak. Edward yelled 'Catch it!' His intentions were, I know, entirely benevolent. He wanted to put it somewhere safe, beyond the garden where war was waged on moles. We rushed after it and I plunged and grabbed it and it slipped through my hands like soap. I can feel it now—soft and dry and warm and so slippery it was gone again at once. Squeaking. We had it once more and again it got away and then it found the dry crumbling earth by the hedge and even as we watched it vanished down into the ground, showering pink earth backwards at us.

I came out of the kitchen garden through the black wrought-iron gate by the quince and past the buddleias and senecios by the iris garden hedge. There was a foam of old-man's-beard over the netting round the tennis lawn, and the grass was ankle-deep. But it always was when we were children; Betty kept geese there, in the war.

I went up the steps and into the iris garden. The iris

4

garden is long and narrow, enclosed by high yew hedges
—ten or twelve feet high—with a shallow canal a couple
of feet wide down the middle leading into a square pool
at one end. It is a quiet, safe, encircled place. There are
water lilies on the canal and the pool, and pale goldfish
beneath, and water-boatmen denting the surface of the
water with thin, splayed legs. This is where we began,
I used to think, the first place of all. There is a photograph of us in one of the albums in the house, sitting
on the grass by the canal. Edward is two years old and
I am one—fat babies sitting in the sun, with our shadows
lying stiffly beside us. Edward is looking straight at the
camera, very solemn and trusting. I am looking to one
side, as though something has caught my eye at the
shadowy edge of the picture. I look cross, or apprehen-
sive. You can see the dark hedge behind us, and nothing
beyond that.

I looked at the goldfish, today, and the neat green fans
of the irises, cut back after flowering, and from time to
time leaves fluttered down from the wisteria and lay on
top of the water, or sank very slowly to the bottom. I
could hear the removal men inside the house: thumps
and shouts and heavy feet walking across bare floors.

I came out into the rose garden, and then through the
other black iron gate under the Japanese cherries and
down on to the terrace under the rose garden wall. The
level of the garden drops here, and the lawn reaches
down to the ha-ha and the field. There is a huge Cedar
of Lebanon, dark and layered, a sculptural tree, and a
sycamore, dripping with pale keys. Mother must have
planted them, once, a careful choice of shape and colour.

They have grown too big now, out of scale with the garden.

There is a lead tank for goldfish just under the wall. It has a statue of a boy holding a dolphin, and a date—1710—and the dolphin's scales, if you look closely, are the wrong way round. Yellow climbing-roses fall over it and there is always a scum of leaves on the water. Once, when I was six, I did a dreadful thing here. Trying to catch the fish with my hands I dislodged the drainage plug at the bottom. The water ran out and the fish flapped hopelessly among the leaves. I fled, aghast, to the house and said I felt ill. They put me to bed. Someone found and rescued the fish before they died, I think. All I remember is lying in the dark, desolate and alone. The tank was empty when I stood by it yesterday—there have been no fish for years—but the emotion came rushing back, like a bad taste. It is called guilt: at six, knowing it for the first time, I felt as though clutched by some disease.

Coming round the side of the house, past the cloak-room and the kitchen and Betty's sitting-room, I heard the rooms echo again to the removal men's tramping feet. There were two vans in the round circle of drive at the front—Pearson and Draper of Minehead. It is a big house, even now it still seems big, curving round from the iris garden at one end to the kitchen yard at the other, rooms packed between—study and drawing-room and dining-room and bedrooms above and then all the back parts, sculleries and pantries and attics. It seemed surprising that two vans would hold all that was in there.

She would sell most of it, Sheila. She had told me that

in her letter, and asked if there was anything I would particularly like. The house would be sold too; she could not manage it any more, at her age. She might go somewhere warm, she thought. Spain, perhaps. She hoped that we would meet before too long. I wrote to say there was nothing I wanted, thank you very much. 'Dear Sheila', I wrote, though I always found it difficult to call her that to her face. I was grown-up, married myself, when father married her. 'Sheila' seemed crudely familiar, to a stranger with grey hair, and there is no accepted word of address for stepmothers. I never knew her well; she came from father's world of bridge-parties and race-meetings.

No, thank you, there was nothing I particularly wanted. Not even the Mah-Jongg set or the lattice-work screen from the drawing-room, or the brass gong-stand in the hall. Or my old desk. Or Edward's. Or the squashy sofa from the playroom. Or our bookcase. I don't need objects.

We never played Mah-Jongg with the Mah-Jongg set, anyway: we didn't know the rules. We invented games of our own, or simply used the tiny ivory counters and sticks to make patterns with, or build houses. They had a strange, cold, ivory smell that I would know again anywhere. My children would like them, I daresay. Maybe I should have said yes, please, to Sheila.

No. I can buy my children a Mah-Jongg set.

I didn't go into the house. The men from Pearson and Draper's came in and out, carrying tables and lamps and rolled-up carpets. I saw the chintz armchair from Betty's room go into the van, and the big dark picture of a storm at sea that hung on the landing, and the flowered water-jugs and basins that the land-girls had in their room down at the stables. I watched all that for a bit, until the men came to sit in a row on the wall by the hydrangeas for their tea-break, and then I went round the side of the house, past the kitchen yard and down the stable drive to the stables. There were cabbages planted out in the patch of ground to the left, by the old cherries, just where there always used to be cabbages, fat, purple ones. There were no cows in the field on the other side, though. Father gave up the farm long ago; he never cared for farming, anyway.

The stables had been built for horses, back when the house was built, in 1900 or so. They were turned over to cows later, during the war, when Medleycott was a proper farm. There is a yard, paved at one end, and the stables enclose it on three sides. The fourth opens into a big chicken-run, with old wooden chicken-houses half-submerged in grass and cow-parsley and stands of nettles. Father used to have Samba shut in the chicken-run, at the times when he banished her from the house. She would lie there, hopeless, a great golden heap of dejection and we would get in with her and feed her biscuits and toast and sit with our arms round her in a tangle of sentiment, hating father. Samba went on loving him, of course. Labradors are natural doormats. Who ever saw a labrador fight back? Terriers, we have now: brisk, resilient dogs.

The chicken-run was choked with nettles, today. I got a stick and beat them down; the sight of that abandoned place annoyed me. In the old days, it was neat and tidy and full of amiable chicken-noises. We used to collect

8

the eggs every evening, after tea. The land-girls would be in their room in the stable-flat and you'd hear them singing and laughing—'I'm flying over ... the white cliffs of Dover ...' Or Susie might be leaning out of the window, drying her hair in the sun. She was always washing her hair.

That's another smell I never smell now, along with the smell of Mah-Jongg pieces. The smell of the inside of a chicken-house, when you've opened up the wooden flap at the back to get the eggs, and there are the nesting-boxes, full of straw, and maybe a warm, cross brown hen, and eggs with feathers sticking to them. I buy my eggs by the half-dozen now, at the supermarket; they are encased in plastic and they never have feathers sticking to them. Nor are they precious. Then, in 1941 or 1942 or 1943 or whichever it was, eggs were rationed. One a week, for most people. More for us, because of keeping our own chickens, but not that many more. We always carried them back to the house walking with unnatural care, looking down at the ground. You couldn't fall, carrying eggs.

There was something I wanted to find, down here at the stables. If it was still here.

It was. Very faint now, pencilled writing on the earthy pink rough-cast of one of the pillars. 'Acre End Farm, Chedzoy.' And a telephone number. I read it through several times, to make sure.

Back at the car, my husband had almost finished the crossword. 'All right? Everything just the same?'

'It was all just the same,' I said.

'Anything more you want to see?'

'Nothing more.' I said.

'There's plenty of time, you know.'

'I'd rather go now. It's getting late.'

We began to drive down the hill.

'One thing,' I said. 'It's funny, but I've always thought —always been quite sure—it was Westonzoyland. It wasn't. It was Chedzoy.'

'What was?'

'The place we ran away to. Edward and I.'

He had to slow up for a tractor on the corner. 'You what?'

'Ran away to.'

'Ran away? From Medleycott? I thought it was such a paradise.'

'It wasn't Medleycott we were running away from, really. It was all very muddled.'

'Explain yourself.'

I'll try. But before that there was a great deal. I'll have to go back to the beginning. And how will I know that what I remember is what actually happened? Like always I have thought it was Westonzoyland, and now I see it was Chedzoy.

2

Remembering is like that. There's what you know happened, and what you think happened. And then there's the business that what you know happened isn't always what you remember. Things are fudged by time; years fuse together. The things that should matter—the stepping-stones that marked the way, the decisions that made one thing happen rather than another—they get forgotten. You are left with islands in a confused and layered landscape, like the random protrusions after a heavy snowfall, the telegraph pole and hump of farm machinery and buried wall. There is time past, and time to come, and time that is continuous, in the head for ever.

I am walking down the lane to Rodhuish, through misty rain, and a woman stops her car to ask the way to Minehead. She winds down the window, and her questioning face is with me still. I do not know who she was, or when it was, but I can see her now. And my first day at school I do not remember at all ... Edward and I are lying in brown autumn bracken up on Croydon Hill, reading, and a glistening green fly crawls across the page of my book. It is still in front of me, veined wings and cockerel-feather sheen. But I forget when, or why, Betty left Medleycott ... I am collecting fossils at Blue Anchor —the grey of the sea welded to the grey of the sky, the fossil a grey whirl on my open palm. But I do not remember the last time I saw Edward before he went to Korea.

People's lives tell a story, I thought once: and then, and next, and then ... But they don't. Nothing so simple. If it's a story at all, then there are two of them, running side by side. What actually happened, and what we remember. Which is more important, I wonder?

Edward was one when I was born. That year, that missing year when he was here and I was not, remained like a small ledge between us, always, as though he stood one step higher on a ladder we were both climbing. And mother died when we were two and three. Edward used to think he could remember her: I knew I didn't. She had a straw hat, he used to say, that she wore in the garden, and it had long brown ribbons hanging down from it, and he remembered her sitting on the rose garden seat wearing this hat. But then one day we were with Betty in the attic turning out an old chest and she took out a hat and said, 'Well, look at that now—there's your mother's old garden hat. Fancy that being here still!' And it didn't have brown ribbons at all, just a kind of pink band round it.

Mother died, and I think there were people who looked after us for a while but who I do not remember, and then there was Betty. Betty had done the cooking, always, and now she took us over too, and the other, shadowy, people went away and we were Betty's affair, with father intruding sometimes, but less and less. We lived in the playroom and in Betty's red-tiled, flour-smelling kitchen and in Betty's sitting-room with the brown wireless crackling to itself on the mantelpiece. And in the garden. The garden was our territory—the space within which we knew the arrangement of every leaf and stone and branch. Beyond the garden was an undefined and forbidden world. And then, somehow, that world resolved itself into the spread of fields and woods and the blue rise of the Brendons and the Quantocks, and we had climbed the gate and were out there, on Croydon Hill and over on Treborough Common and down in the Luxborough valley, and the world had stretched and stretched like elastic and we were making free with it, owning it, occupying it.

Betty, tethered to her kitchen, let us loose like small animals. We came and went as we pleased, restricted only by a few rules. No playing in the stream unless Sandy or someone was nearby. No climbing the chestnut trees. Eat no berries without asking. Shut all gates. Be back in time for lunch. Or tea. Or supper. Within those confines, do as you like and don't get in people's way.

And so, through those years of being five, and six, and seven, we were in the garden, making camps in the spinney and fishing for tadpoles in the ponds and trailing round the kitchen garden after Sandy, the gardener, while Sandy earthed up potatoes and hoed the onion beds and pruned the cordon apples. 'You run down the potting-shed and get me four flower-pots,' said Sandy. 'Four mind.' And we trotted up and down the grass paths and wheeled the big wooden barrow and helped ourselves to raffia and pea-sticks for building houses.

We are in the drawing-room, and Betty and Sandy are there too, which is not how things usually are, and father is standing by the fire-place and we are to sit quietly on the sofa and not talk. I fidget and am shushed by Betty. A man with a thin voice talks out of the wireless: 'May God bless you all,' he says, and they play 'God Save the King'. The sun makes a yellow patch on the carpet and I stare at it and words go round and round in my head from the record we have got in the playroom: 'Don't go down to the woods today ... if you go down to the woods today, you're in for a big surprise.'

Later, I ask Betty if the war is going to be here at Medleycott, and she does not answer.

Father went away almost at once, after war was declared. He joined the Somerset Light Infantry and was posted up to Scotland and we hardly missed him at all. We did not know him very well. His part of the house, beyond the glass door on the upstairs landing, had thick carpets and smelt of polish and you had to be careful not to knock over little wobbly tables and flower-vases. We went there, but it was not our territory. Our territory was the back landing, where the thick carpets ended and the rush matting began, and the downstairs part beyond the swing door, the red-tiled pantry and passage and kitchen. On Sundays we wore best clothes and had lunch with father in the dining-room, and father teased us because that was the only way he knew to talk to children, and sometimes he shouted at Edward because Edward was a boy and boys must be kept in order.

Edward was afraid of father.

With father gone, Betty shut up most of the house. 'No point in blacking-out what nobody's going to use,' she said, and in the yard outside the kitchen we stirred glorious inky mush in the cattle-troughs and dyed old sheets for black-out curtains. And the sheets, spread out to dry in the sun on the lawn, left the grass chequered with black patches, and we played Tom Tiddler's Ground on and off the patches and screamed ourselves hoarse because with father gone there was no one to tell us to stop that row in my garden.

Mr Pitt from Rodhuish came bobbing down the drive on his bike with the bike lamp all blued over and his Air Raid Warden armband on, to look at our blackout, and Betty gave him a cup of tea in the kitchen and they talked about evacuees and rationing and war efforts and we hung about by the Aga, warming ourselves and not understanding. Mr Pitt let Edward put his tin hat on and Edward said, 'How soon will the Germans start dropping bombs on Rodhuish?'

'They've not let me know, young man,' said Mr Pitt, and he asked Betty if she'd be off to work in a munitions factory and Betty grinned and said she was in a reserved occupation and pointed at us, and Mr Pitt told her about the Franklin girls going off to make aeroplanes in Sheffield and their mother being left single-handed on the farm with no one but the old man.

Sandy was too old to join the army. 'I done my bit,' he said, 'last time round.' Jim went, though, who helped

Tom Fletcher. Medleycott was partly a farm, and Tom Fletcher ran the farm part for father. Father called himself a farmer, but he did not do much farming. He was often away for days on end, and it was Tom Fletcher who decided when to start hay-making and how many heifers to take to Washford market. Now, Tom Fletcher was reserved, too. A stockman was too important to send away for a soldier. He became too busy to talk to us any more and Betty was to look after the chickens. We were to help: that would be our war work. Pompous with self-importance, we carried the steaming chicken-mash down to the stable-yard and collected the eggs. Betty rummaged in the attics for mattresses and bolsters and we began to hear the word 'land-girl'.

'What's a land-girl?' said Edward, and Betty, flashing past with table-lamps and pillow-cases, snapped, 'You'll find out soon enough.'

We knew our Hans Andersen and our *Tales of Ancient Greece*. Like water-nymphs, we decided, or tree-spirits. Elemental, elusive creatures. We waited, hopefully, for them to appear.

The quoit flips against the sky. I throw it as high as I can and it flips and spins and comes down too fast to catch. I chant as I throw it: 'Immunization and evacuation and mobilization *and* immunization and evacuation and mobilization.' These are the words that crackle through Betty's wireless in the kitchen at breakfast. I do not know what they mean but they are good words. 'Conscription,' I yell at the sky, and miss the quoit again.

*   *   *

There was a war on, people said. They said it like a refrain, like 'touchwood' or 'cross-my-heart', so that you stopped hearing it. There was a war on, so you couldn't have lots of sweets any more, just one sixpenny bar of chocolate a week, and no more oranges or bananas. There was a war on, so we mustn't waste things because there won't be any more where that came from. There was a war on so Betty couldn't go to Minehead to the pictures on Saturday night because there was no petrol for the car, at least not for things like cinemas. There was a war on so we had to keep a bucket of sand inside the kitchen door in case of incendiary bombs and Sandy dropped his cigarette ends into it, day by day, till it was more cigarette than sand.

There was a war on, but the Somerset hills encircled the house and the garden just as they always had done, and the pink lanes tipped up and down between the high hedges full of toadflax and foxgloves. Mushrooms popped up overnight in the field by the stream and one of the cows had twin calves, shiny brown like conkers. Edward's loose front tooth came out in church one Sunday morning and he sucked it like a sweet till the end of the service. I sat all one day in the dry gloom of the yew hedge with the *Just So Stories*, resolved to read long words like Edward could. And came out triumphant, reading aloud to Sandy across the lettuces. 'Very nice, Jane,' says Sandy, pricking out seedlings. 'You try this seed-packet now.' And I glow with pride, reading seed-packets and the lawn-mower's guarantee and Sandy's *Daily Mirror*.

'Who wants a ride to Washford?' said Tom Fletcher and, exulting, we packed into the back of the farm truck, with our hair tidied in case we saw anyone. The land-girls were arriving, and had to be met at the station. Tom did errands on the way: the blacksmith, to see about repairing a scythe, the corn merchant, about cattle-food, and the White Horse, about something that kept Tom inside for five minutes or so and brought him out wiping his mouth with the back of his hand, in a good mood. He let Edward steer the truck along the straight bit past Cleeve Abbey, and not me. Driving cars was man's work. But I, dreaming about land-girls, did not really mind. The truck crawled at not much more than horse-pace and Tom talked to it like he talked to cows and horses, encouraging it up the hills and slanging it if he thought it wasn't trying.

The Taunton train was late. 'That'll be the London connection,' said Tom knowingly. 'All cock-eyed they are these days,' and we nodded, as though we knew all about the unreliable ways of London trains. And then at last the distant emptiness of the track was plugged with move-ment and a plume of blue smoke and then the train was there, letting out Mrs Sampson with her shopping and her niece from Crowcombe and two soldiers and Tessie Armstrong.

And the land-girls. They wore creased grey flannel coats and skirts and they carried brown suitcases and they were perfectly ordinary. They were called Pam and Susie. Mute with disappointment, I trailed behind them to the car. Edward, who had forgotten our expectations, was being polite and opening doors and carrying things. Tom Fletcher had put on a new voice for them, gruff and a bit stern, as though they might get out of hand. They sat

18

in the back of the van talking in voices that seemed to us like the voices of foreigners, because they came from Birmingham and we had never heard anything but the voices of West Somerset, Betty's and Sandy's and Tom's (and father's, which was different, of course, and those of aunts and cousins which were like father's, and our own, which used to be like that but were now more like Betty's). They exclaimed about the lanes and the fields and the trees and the flowers in the hedges. It's really nice down here, they said, really beautiful, and Tom made the gears crash on the corner and said you wait till you seen it five o'clock of a winter morning.

The land-girls were installed in the flat over the stables and appeared in the kitchen for tea wearing baggy brown breeches and green jerseys and ridiculous hats with badges, which we never saw again. Sandy and Tom Fletcher and old Roberts from Roadwater who came up now to help with the cows laughed fit to burst. And there began then and there the daily routine of teasing the land-girls, who were well able to defend themselves. Remarks flew back and forth, from then till the end of the war, across the kitchen table and over hedges and under the muddy bellies of cows. Remarks about who was that I saw you with in the lane last night and you watch out Mr Fletcher or I'll be telling your wife about you and that's a spade you're using girl not a bloody broom.

Pam and Susie were nice.

And Betty was king of the castle. The world had contracted, with father going away and the house all shut up and dust-sheeted, but at the same time it had expanded. The kitchen was the hub of an empire that included everyone working on the farm and more besides—everyone who came down the drive, the postman and the district nurse and the neighbours. Everyone stopped off for tea and gossip, and we sat down to dinner in the middle of the day round the kitchen table, half a dozen or more, with Betty standing at the door to see the men left their boots outside. And nobody cared any more about dogs being kept outside so Samba lived with us now, in slumbering joy in front of the Aga or stretched out on the playroom sofa, easing us off with a large golden rump. And even Jip, the farm collie, got as far as the kitchen, and lay muddy and tired under the table with no one saying anything.

Autumn. The hedge outside the gate has blossomed with spider-webs. All over, they are, from top to bottom, multi-faceted, slung between blackberry sprays or tacked to the dried heads of cow-parsley. Some lead into deep funnels that plunge into the depths of the hedge, and down there lurk malevolent presences that will come groping up after a probing twig. We squat on our haunches, absorbed; we are spider experts, classifying, investigating. We loom over the intense life of the hedge, huge, detached presences, attending now to this, now to that. Now to this dainty, scarlet-bodied creature with her complex creation between two trails of ivy, now to this tattered battlefield draped across the docks. 'Look!' says Edward, and we are motionless spectators of ambush and slaughter.

*   *   *

There had been a time when a Miss Cartland came from Minehead to give us lessons. We sat on either side of her at the playroom table and made pot-hooks in exercise books, and read dull stories aloud. But the war put an end to Miss Cartland, along with sweets and oranges and Betty's Saturdays at the cinema. I cannot remember, as I said before, how we first went to school, but it happened. One day we were free and busy in the garden, the next we were bundled into clean clothes and standing doleful at the top of the lane, either side of Betty, to be put on the school bus down to Washford.

Remembering is strange in another way, too—the things that you did over and over again, day after day, reduce themselves to a single, hazy, long-drawn-out moment. I sit at a desk with inky grooves, between Linda Simmons and Dawn Hosegood, and a bluebottle buzzes high up against the window, and the old black stove wheezes (it is very hot—the big boys spit on it at play-time and their spit scuds off in white balls) and Mrs Laycock is chalking something on the board and we copy it carefully, in best writing, into exercise books with coarse, grainy wartime paper. That was school—that, and the school bus squeezing through the summer growth of the lanes, cow-parsley and meadowsweet brushing the windows. There was one class and one teacher. One class for everybody from five-year-olds to lusty boys of twelve who would be off home at dinner to help their dads on the farm. And Mrs Laycock in always the same flowery dress through which you could see the armour-plating of her stays. We did History and Geography and Arithmetic and we traced maps of the world and coloured pink the bits that belonged to England. We learned poems by heart and said them to Mrs Laycock with our heads tilted backwards and our hands clasped behind us, and we made raffia mats for Handicrafts and sometimes we went down to the field beside the stream and did Nature Study. All that throughout a single, long, indistinct day that is a fusion of a hundred, three hundred, similar days.

School did not intrude into Medleycott. Washford was too far for children from there to visit us. At home, we had only David. David was Mr Pitt's son from down in Rodhuish. He was twenty days older than Edward, and they seemed, together, so unalike as to be some illustration of opposing racial types: David stolidly Anglo-Saxon, large-boned, pink-cheeked, thatched with thick pale hair—Edward thin, angular, worried-looking. They got on excellently. Meeting David in the lane or the fields, we would join forces until David chose to go his own way again, and from time to time he would visit us in the garden, but not if father was at home. At the sight of father he would melt away through the nearest gate or hedge. We traded our assets for David's—tadpoling in our ponds in exchange for David's right of access to a new litter of pigs in his father's farmyard; jumping down our ha-ha, foraging in our kitchen garden, in return for watching (at a respectful distance) the old bull at work. There was a perfect equality about our different advantages. Like amicable neighbouring tribes, we examined and assessed and exchanged.

And, when the evacuees came, we fell into a natural alliance. They swarmed into David's world overnight, two girls and a boy, respectively older and younger than we were, invading David's territory down in Rodhuish, throwing stones into the pond, climbing the trees in the orchard, swinging on David's gates. And David, flabbergasted and at a loss how to respond, came to us for support. They were billeted at the Dawson's cottage— two lank-haired girls and a small boy, all three with socks that tumbled in corrugations around their ankles and bundled clothes that did not fit them. We could not understand their London accents and they were baffled by ours. 'Eh?' they said, 'Eh?' and for a morning we circled each other like wary dogs, each side establishing credentials. David and Edward, climbing trees, running along walls, showed off with abandon; Iris and Lena, mothering their small brother, brandishing their advantage of superior age, bravely claimed for themselves a place in this remote and alien world to which they had been brought by strangers. Years later, I found myself in the Stepney from which they had come—what was left of it after the Blitz—and realized their courage. Rodhuish must have seemed like a different planet. By the end of the day we had achieved a relationship, and lived more or less in peace thereafter.

And somewhere else, in London and over there in France, in the world of the voices that read the nine o'clock news out of Betty's wireless, other things were happening. The grown-ups used the same words over and over again: Dunkirk, General de Gaulle, Blitz. We must Dig for Victory, and Sandy was in the Home Guard and did something on Treborough Common called manoeuvres, and in the school playground the boys played Spitfires and Hurricanes and no one wanted to be the Luftwaffe.

3

Father came home on leave. The Washford taxi brought
him up from the station because the Rover was put away
in the garage till the end of the war. He was wearing
uniform, with a shiny brown belt across his chest and a
brown leather stick that lay across the gong-stand till he
went away again. We hung round a bit, interested, and
father joked at us in the too-loud voice he always used
with us, and after a bit we went away and got on with
the game we had been playing down in the spinney before
he came.

We had Sunday dinner with father in the dining-room.
Betty went backwards and forwards with dishes and
through the swing door came puffs of noise from the
kitchen, Pam and Susie laughing. Father didn't like the
way Edward held his knife and was cross; Edward
stared at the knife and tried to hold it other ways and
gravy spilled on the cloth.

'Teaching you anything down at Washford, are they?'
said father, and we said yes, they were.

'Seven times eight?' said father. 'Come along, now.'
And we rummaged in our heads, frantic, and Edward
came up with something which would do, it seemed,

25

because father made no comment.

We told him more about what we did at school, and father interrupted Edward in the middle of a sentence and said, 'Talk proper English, Edward, can't you.'

Edward starts again, bewildered, 'We has our dinner and then ...'

'Have,' says father, 'have, for heaven's sake. And you don't have dinner in the middle of the day, do you?' We are at a loss, because you do, and we cannot understand what he means about this talking, so we do not say any more, to be on the safe side.

Monday, father goes away again, back up to Scotland to teach people to drive tanks, and Betty lets Samba out out of the chicken run and we have dinner with Pam and Susie in the kitchen again and everybody laughs a lot.

We sat on a gate and watched men from the County Council take down the signpost at the end of the lane. The familiar three fingers pointing up, down, and to Medleycott were stacked in the back of a lorry piled with other posts, a tangle of Watchet, Dunster, Carhampton and Withycombe. What, we asked, did they want them for?

And were told.

'No good showing the Germans how to get theirselves about, is it? Got to confuse them, haven't we? Put them wrong?'

'Suppose,' said Edward intensely, 'they ask people the way?'

'You don't tell no one. Not unless you know them for local.'

'When will they come?'

'Could be any time now, they reckon.'

'They'll not come,' said one of the men, older than the others. He snapped, it seemed to make him angry, this speculation. He shouted at the others, who were not much more than schoolboys, telling them to get a move on, and the lorry went away.

And we went home, important with information, to tell the grown-ups, who already knew, it seemed. 'Invasion', it was—another of these words that had buzzed around us and that we had not listened to, like you don't listen to the bluebottle on the window that is always there. The Germans might come. They might come here, into our fields and lanes, dropping out of the summer skies on the ends of parachutes, like so many floating mushrooms. To this day, seeing a box of mushrooms in a greengrocer's, I am taken back to that summer, standing on the lawn with my head tilted backwards staring up at those blue and white skies out of which the Germans would come, into our garden and our lane and our ten-acre field.

And from which we would misdirect them. Ah, we'd scupper them, pitched down into the anonymity of our signpostless, maze-like Somerset lanes, baffling even to one born and bred five miles away. 'London,' we would say, pointing west, and send them storming along to Exeter and Land's End. We hugged ourselves with satisfaction—oh, we'd settle their hash, we'd cook their goose, that we would. We practised, sitting on the drive gate, staring hopefully down the lane up which they would come, up from Rodhuish, humping their rifles and their kit bags, questioning us in their broken English.

'S'pose they've got compasses?' said Edward. We looked at each other in alarm. 'And maps. You can work out where you are, on a map, if you know where north and south are, from the hills and roads and things.'

Horrified, we took the problem to Sandy, digging at the top of the kitchen garden. He wiped his hands on his corduroys, and stared down at us, a drip of moisture gleaming at the tip of his nose.

'What's the trouble, then?'

We explained, breathless.

Sandy considered, scraping earth off the fork with the toe of his boot.

'They'll not have time, will they?' he said at last. 'Not with the pill-box up at the top, and me and young Taylor in it, most likely. They'll not be bothered with paper-work at a time like that—they'd have to get on the move sharpish, not hang around with maps and that. Anyway,' he added as an afterthought, 'they'd have maps in German, wouldn't they? That wouldn't be any good to 'em.'

Satisfied, we went away, and perfected our schemes with a mobile trip-wire across the entrance to the drive. That would floor them, in every sense.

It is tadpole time. In the pond, the goldfish slide under the lily-pads. The sides of the pond grow a thick fur of green weed, and on to the weed are latched tadpoles by the hundred, grazing away there an inch or two below the surface, with glistening bulbous heads and tails in perpetual motion. We lie on our faces, our bodies cold

against the flagstones, and stare down at them, so close
that our breath dents the water, and they chomp away
unaware. We dip our hands in and scoop them out in
ones and twos, and they skirmish in the pink ponds of
our hands, round and round, frantic, tickling, their eyes
and panting mouths revealed. We maroon them on lily-
pads, thrashing in a drop of water, and then relent: we
dunk the pads and watch the tadpoles' desperate plunge
downwards to the concealing mud. They sound, minia-
ture, tormented whales, and the pond is empty. Down
in the mud, black tails quiver.

The Germans didn't come. People stopped expecting
them and the pill-box at the top of the hill grew a fringe
of weeds around its base and strangers in the lanes were
no longer treated to a grim and suspicious silence. There
were soldiers encamped up on Treborough Common;
their lorries and motor-bikes rattled past the drive gates.
Saturdays, there were dances down at the village hall and
on Friday evenings Pam and Susie washed their hair
and dried it by the Aga and ironed their frocks on the
landing outside the playroom and we joined in the game
of teasing the land-girls.
'What's your boyfriend's name, Susie?'
'What do you know about boyfriends at your age, I'd
like to know.'
'Has he kissed you, Susie?'
Until Susie has had enough and chases us out into the
yard and we run round shrieking in the half-dark and
Samba is barking and jumping up and down and Betty
has to come out and fetch us in for bed.

Once, Betty took us down to the village just for the first half-hour of the dance, just to see, just for a special treat. It was like Christmas, birthdays, going away for a holiday. Out of the grassy, leafy darkness of the lane and into the bright, noisy, peopled village hall with the girls all round the walls in tidy frocks and lipstick just put on and hair neat-rolled round a hidden stocking (we know, we have seen what Pam and Susie do). And there were the soldiers, in thick gritty khaki uniforms and hair sleeked back, smoking, eyeing ...

Betty arranged us by the tea-urns and went off to give a hand with the sandwiches. At the other end, beyond the stage, there was a bar, and, we were given to understand, wickedness. We were to stay put where we'd been told and not go running off.

'There's Mrs Taylor's Linda.'

'There's Minnie Dixon.'

'There's Pam and Susie.'

And there, after a while, was Betty, pink in the face, dancing with a soldier who wore his hat threaded through the tab on his shoulder and held her clamped stiff to his middle. The loudspeakers magnified the wheeze and scratch of the gramophone, the room shuffled and gyrated, there was a smell of sweat, and hair-oil, and scented soap.

'The one Betty's got is grander than the one Susie's got,' said Edward.

'Why?'

'He's got three stripe things.'

'Susie's has a nicer face.'

We had sausage rolls and orangeade. It was nine o'clock

at night. We were part of the dance, seeing it, being there. It was unearthly.

'Let's go outside,' I said, carried away.

'We mustn't.'

'Other people are.'

The other people, though, were going off into the bushy blackness of the recreation ground, in twos, one soldier to one girl, khaki arms round flowered cotton waists. Uncertainly, we hung around the steps at the back of the hall, where shredded light streamed out through the shutters, in defiance of the blackout. A soldier sat on the top step, smoking. We admired him through the gloom and, presently, shuffled our bottoms sideways along the step until we were sitting three in a row.

'Hello.'

'Hello, there.'

He didn't seem to be enjoying himself, the soldier.

Edward said, politely, 'Are you having a nice time?'

'It'll do, I suppose, son,' said the soldier.

There was a silence. The soldier lit another cigarette off the end of the one he was smoking. Edward whispered to me and I nodded. The problem seemed clear enough.

'We know a girl you could dance with,' said Edward. 'She's called Pam and she's very nice. She's a bit fat,' he added, laying all his cards on the table. 'But not all that fat, and I should think she's quite pretty.'

The soldier laughed. He laughed for quite a long

time and gave Edward a pat on the back and then he said, 'Thanks very much, son—but no thanks all the same. No offence meant, eh?'

'Don't you like girls?' said Edward.

'I like girls all right. But not just any girl, see.'

There were scufflings in the recreation ground, giggles, little shrieks. People trotted up and down the steps and the whole hall seemed to throb a little with the thump-thump-thump of the music.

'Matter of fact,' said the soldier, 'I was thinking about my old woman. My wife.'

Ah. We nodded.

'Where is she?' I said.

'A long way away,' said the soldier. 'Too damn far away, that's what.' He began to whistle, a quiet, breathy kind of whistling.

'Why don't you go and see her?' said Edward encouragingly.

'Because,' said the soldier, 'there's a war on, that I didn't ever ask to get lumbered with. But I am lumbered with it, so I'm sat here and my wife's way up there, and that's the way it is, and it's a right mess, as far as I'm concerned.' He got up and threw the cigarette away into the darkness. 'Well, I think I'll push off. Cheerio.'

'Cheerio,' we said.

And the soldier went away and we went back into the hall and sat on chairs that thumped softly underneath us in time to the music, and everything became a little blurred and hazy and after a while Betty came and bustled us away into the back of Mr Feather's car to be taken home. We were asleep before we got there and Mr

32

Feather, they said next day, had to help Betty carry us upstairs.

The dance, like a stone thown in a pond, generated disturbances which in turn generated other disturbances ... Betty had a tiff with her old enemy, Mrs Curry from the pub, to do with an exchange of views about the refreshments, and Mrs Curry mentioned to father next time he came on leave that she'd seen us down at the village hall, Saturday night. And father said things to Betty in the kitchen, with the doors shut, but in a loud voice, and Betty came out and went into her sitting-room with her eyes all red and her mouth funny, and said not to bother her for a bit.

And we never went to the village hall on a Saturday night again.

Nor did we ever see the soldier. But Edward, playing halma with Betty at the kitchen table chants, 'I'm the war, and I'm putting all the red ones *there* and the black ones *there* and this is the soldier on the step and he's got to go *there* and this is Pam and Susie and they've got to be *here*.'

And Betty says, 'You stop your yammering on and make a move or I'm off to do the potatoes.'

The Germans didn't come, but there were strangers about, nonetheless. There were Italian prisoners-of-war working on Mr Pitt's farm. Harvesting in the steep-sloping Croydon fields, they sang: huge, passionate and unfamiliar songs, not at all like the warbling of Pam and Susie, or Betty's good-mood humming in the kitchen. Edward, in particular, was fascinated. We hung over a gate and listened with David to a lush male voice yearning across the stubble.

'My dad says less noise and more muscle and we'd get the sixteen-acre cut a bit quicker,' said David.

But Edward said, 'It's nice, the singing.'

'They gave me toffees,' said David, 'last week.'

And they gave us toffees too, with much smiling and white teeth in dark faces, and patting of us, so that we were embarrassed and did not know what we should do. 'Bambini,' they said. 'Aie, bambini ...' And we told Betty about them and she said they were a long way from home and it didn't do any harm to show a bit of friendliness.

Other strangers there were too, cruising our lanes and coming out of our village shop. Men from the Ministry, in shiny shoes and un-country clothes, and inspectors of this and that, and soldiers, and people from elsewhere come down for the duration, stopping with aunts and sisters, or just plain billeted like the evacuees.

And one day, in the village shop, there was Mike, buying cigarettes. I can see him now—and I can smell the shop. It is a generic smell—the smell of all village shops. I have met it since—in Suffolk, in Glamorgan, in Westmorland—and each time it has sent me back to Roadwater, among the biscuits and cards of elastic and boxes of envelopes. A symposium of smells, it is— chocolate; soap; candles; matches; apples; brown envelopes.

'Brown envelopes don't smell,' says Edward, thirty years ago, and I say passionately yes they do and we argue, trudging up the hill eating the chocolate ration that we had been going to save up to gorge after tea, lick by lick, in front of the fire.

We would have been getting our chocolate ration the first time we met Mike. And thus we heard him talking to Annie Simpson in the shop about looking for a room and thus we went home and reported to Betty, as we reported everything, and thus, in the end, Mike came to live in our attic. But there was more to it than that, even then. Nothing much, just that curious response, which must be physical in some way or maybe mysteriously spiritual, because it can come even before speech, which tells you a person is sympathetic, someone you will like. And so, even without conversation, we knew that this young man we had never seen before, buying his twenty cigarettes from Annie Simpson, was on our side, was a potential friend.

Mike was a conchie. 'A what?' said Edward, fork half-way to mouth, and for once we attend to an explanation, because, somehow, we feel involved.

'A conscientious objector,' said Betty. 'And don't think you're leaving that corned beef, Edward, because you're not. That's someone that doesn't believe in fighting so they're not called up but they've got to do war work. Go down the mines or on the land.'

And the status provoked discussion. People had opinions, it seemed, about conchies.

'I dunno,' said Susie, 'I think they should have to join up. I mean, if everyone felt like that ...'

'There'd be no wars, would there?' said Betty tartly.

'I mean, our soldiers are fighting for them too, aren't they, whether they want people fighting for them or not.'

'It's their religion, isn't it, some of them?'

'Bolshies,' said Sandy darkly.

'It's not how I'd see things,' said Betty, 'not with Hitler. But everyone's entitled to their opinion.'

'They gave them white feathers, last time,' said Sandy, 'the women did. For cowardice, see.'

And that, for some reason, annoyed Betty and maybe was the random shove that sets moving one series of events rather than another. If Sandy hadn't said that, put Betty obscurely and indefinably in favour of Mike, maybe she wouldn't have let it be known down in the village that there was an attic going spare up at Medleycott, and maybe the billeting officer (Mr Palmer, from Luxborough) wouldn't have come to see about it and maybe Mike wouldn't have moved in, with his sparse possessions—work-clothes, best shirt and trousers for Sundays, his books—glad to be away from Cliffe Farm, where he was still to work but where the only place for him to sleep was a camp-bed in the scullery. And maybe, later, much later, we wouldn't have walked away out of the drive gates with one pound five and six and some apples.

'Ask God for the war to end soon,' says Betty. She sits on the bed, her legs, in thick lisle stockings, planted firmly on the lino, and we kneel each side of her, resentful, because we are too old, we think, for this public praying—or maybe any praying. But Betty is C. of E., strict, so we must or she will be put out and that is worse than the praying. So we kneel either side of her and say 'Our Father' and I stare at the wrinkles in her stockings and think of bark on trees, all ribbed and grooved, and Edward, I can see if I slant my eyes, is picking threads out of the blanket. Betty trims her nails with a file, and hums to herself. 'Please God,' we chant, 'make the war end soon.' And when we are done we get into bed with flying leaps, so that the beds skid across the floor.

4

Mike was twenty. We had married him, in our minds, to Susie, but Susie was twenty-three, which made Mike no good to her at all, not when there were soldiers on Treborough Common. So Pam and Susie teased Mike and Mike grinned and didn't care and Betty piled food high on his plate because he was too thin. And even Sandy, who knew what he felt about conchies, said he was a nice enough lad, one way and another, when all was said and done.

Mike found the violin in the attic.

'Good Lord,' he said. 'It works.' And he held the thing under his chin, like people in pictures, and capered about with it, carving lush and wild sounds and leaning over us, singing into our ears, a soaring song like the Italian prisoners sang up on Croydon Hill. I had never heard anything so funny—I hugged myself with delight, begged him to go on. But Edward was not amused. He had gone all intense, like a dog pointing.

'How do you know how to do it? How does it work? Show me.'

And Mike, amiable, showed. 'Right. Hand round here, chin tucked in. We need a half-size really, but we can't have a half-size, so you'll have to have elastic arms. Now, bow like this, in the other hand ...'

And then, in Mike's room, we learned that there was another kind of pot-hooks for another kind of language, and books were written in this language too, and Mike knew all about them. Edward sat on the edge of Mike's bed, absorbed, and copied these extended commas, upside-down and right-way up, rows and rows of them, and I was bored and left-out.

'That's what I'd be doing,' said Mike, lying on the bed, hands behind head, 'if jolly old Hitler hadn't mucked things up.'

Mike had been at college, studying music, and would have gone on to do more studying and perhaps be a teacher.

'I don't suppose you've got a piano tucked away some-where too? No, that would have been too good to be true.'

'Why didn't you want to be a soldier, Mike?' Me, fiddling with Mike's picture of his mother and father, his two sisters, the dog.

'I didn't want to fight people. Kill them.'

'Even if the other person's as wicked as Hitler?' Edward, making treble clefs, intent.

'Even then.'

'Would you if they came here? Fight the Germans?' Me, looking at Mike's books. They have funny names: *Cold Comfort Farm*, *Chrome Yellow*, little thin books with just poems in them.

'I don't know,' said Mike, 'that's what I don't really know.'

'If they were going to kill us and Betty and Pam and Susie?' Edward, completing his treble clefs, moving on to a flourish, a fistful of notes from one of Mike's books. 'Andante,' he copies, in best writing.

'Mmm,' said Mike. 'That's the problem, isn't it?'

'I expect you would, really. Do you mind people calling you conchie?' Me, seeing Betty out of the window. She has been in the kitchen garden, getting vegetables— it must be nearly supper time.

'I'd better not mind, had I?' said Mike.

'Better than getting killed.' Edward, frowning at his blunted pencil, licking the point.

'Right,' said Mike. 'Music class over. That'll be one guinea each, payment in cash only.'

And later, in the playroom, Edward holds the violin again, like Mike showed, and scrapes. It is a dismal sound. It bears little relation to the noise Mike made, and less still to the noises, scrawny but designed, that come from the tulip-mouth of father's gramophone. Something is dreadfully wrong. He tries again, and the scrape is different, and fractionally, marginally more endurable. And he tries again. And again and again and again.

There was harvest, and everyone worked till after it was dark, and Mike had blisters on his hands and walked jerkily, like an old man, from stiffness.

'Breaking you in, then, are they?' said Sandy, complacent, but Betty let Mike have more than his ration of hot water for baths, and there was trouble with Pam and Susie. Pam painted a red line on the bath and no one was to go above it, everyone to be on their honour. Sandy threatened to come up and look through the keyhole, and there was much to-and-fro with the girls across the kitchen table. Mike never joined in this, but he would grin hugely, enjoying it.

And the year slid, somehow, into winter. The hot, harvest, blackberry days were gone and we were into November: white skies, dark spiny trees, hot toast for tea, cold hands, feet, noses. Darkness as we feed the chickens, the stable drive pale-fringed with grasses, the landscape huddled under a violet sky, the fields peppered with snow that fell this morning and melted too soon to be any use to us. Winter mud creeping over paths and up through grass. Birds spraying from the dark and wintry hedges.

'I like Mike. I like Mike next best to Sandy. No, equal best.'

'And Tom Dixon?'

We thought about this, anxiously.

'Equal best to Sandy and Tom Dixon. And Betty,' said Edward.

'When she's not cross.'

Edward, chewing grasses, said, 'I think Mike's brave.'

'Brave?'

'It's brave doing something different from what everyone thinks you ought to do. He doesn't like it when they call him conchie—he pretends he doesn't mind, but he does.'

'He sits by himself when they have their sandwiches. He sits by another bit of the hedge.'

'I know. It's a different kind of brave from soldiers.'

'Betty says father's got leave for Christmas.'

'I know.'

The hedges are draped with old-man's-beard, a grey tide; everything is buff and fawn and brown; the grass is freckled with fallen leaves; the cows are in for the winter. In four weeks it will be Christmas. We count the days and groan: four weeks is too long, anticipation will not stretch that far. We climb the gate by the big oak, and balance along the wall, pushing each other, and forget about Christmas.

We did not see all that much of Mike. Going back— remembering—he is not a constant presence, like Betty and Sandy and the land-girls. But when he is there he is forcefully there, so that I hear his voice still (a flat London voice, not a bit like the land-girls' Birmingham, but not a bit like the London voices of the evacuees either, which is puzzling), and see his thin bony face and knobby limbs, always, it seemed, flung down somewhere in exhaustion—on beds, haystacks, verges. He bicycled away in the dawn to work all day at Cliffe Farm, over the other side of the Roadwater valley, and back late to eat and sleep. Only Sundays was he at Medleycott.

He didn't come to church. In Rodhuish, on Sunday mornings, tranced in the praying, singing, whitewash-and-stone familiarity of the place, we reflected upon this, studying in boredom the known, always-known, faces and backs of heads. Everyone went to church. You only didn't go to church if you were ill, or harvesting. Didn't Betty mind?

'Mike didn't come to church,' we said.

'He's got no call to,' said Betty shortly. 'He's got his own faith. He's a Quaker.'

And we, who had never known anyone thus set apart, were impressed. It increased his exoticism still more—being a C.O. (this, we have found, is what conchies are called, less rudely), able to play the violin, and now a Quaker too. We are very proud of him, and boast to David.

'We know somebody who's a Quaker.'

'Oh, ay?' says David. 'Where's he from, then?'

'London.'

'What country?' says David patiently. 'Like a Frenchie comes from France.'

There is a flaw in this somewhere. We see that we have got out of our depth, and change the subject.

We are feeding birds in the kitchen garden. It has snowed in the night and the events of the morning are mapped out between the back door and the garage and the stable drive—blue furrows where Sandy has come on his bike, flurry where he has got off and leaned the bike against the wall, then his boot-prints going to the tap, circle mark of bucket set down, boot-prints going away to stables ... A skitter of round dabs where Samba has come out and run round barking, tiny arrow-trails that the birds have left, small and large. We scrumble the soft innards from the loaf and hold it high above us and now it snows bread upon the snow—soft, flaking, drifting bread. We retire behind the water-butt and fondly watch as they come down—sparrows and tits and an acrimonious robin and a dunnock foraging apart from

43

the rest, shuffling among the leaves. We feel benign and munificent; they need us, what would they do without us?

Christmas came and went, and father with it. He had three days' leave, and arrived, bringing presents and dissension.

'Father won't see Mike,' I said to Betty. Mike was going home for Christmas.

'Just as well, I daresay.'

'Why, Betty?'

'Just as well—that's all. You never know, with him. And I'd leave the subject alone, if I was you.'

'Not talk about Mike?'

'That's it.'

We didn't. But we had learned to be cautious with father. Circumspect. Like when you were in the field where Mr Pitt kept his bull you skirted round the edges, stayed within reach of the gate. With father, we stuck to things we knew from experience did not provoke those sudden, bewildering flights of anger.

He gave me a doll and Edward a box of soldiers. Some of the soldiers lay on their stomachs, aiming rifles. Others stood, humped under equipment, armed to the teeth. There was also a toy cannon, to the same scale, that fired match-sticks. Edward lined them up on the playroom window-sill and moved them here and there like figures on a chess-board. 'Bang-bang,' he said, dutifully, 'bang-bang.' After father had gone they went on standing there, in frozen combat, until after a few weeks they were furry with dust and Betty swept them into the toy-chest. I never saw them again.

Pam and Susie had gone home too, back to Birmingham and their families, eggs packed into their cases wrapped around with stockings and jerseys, a chicken each in a brown carrier bag, plucked and drawn by Betty. 'Mum'll go mad,' said Susie. 'A chicken! It's like taking home the crown jewels.'

And we had chicken too, for Christmas dinner, sitting uneasy in best clothes at the dining-room table, with Betty far away in the kitchen. There had been trouble about Samba. Father had discovered that she lived now in the house and had taken her himself down to the stables where dogs, it seemed, belonged, and tied her up there. There, we knew, she was desolate in straw and darkness, yearning for the Aga and under-table scraps. We ate our chicken and mourned and said, 'Yes,' and 'No,' when father asked us questions. Later, we escaped to Betty and played Demon Patience with riotous noise and ate real toffee Betty made with saved-up sugar ration.

As soon as father had gone we brought Samba up from the stables.

'You did that, mind,' said Betty, 'not me.'

'He won't know, anyway.'

Edward, though, was guilty. He kept hunching his nose, a nervous twitch, in the way that he did when anxious.

'Do stop doing that thing with your nose,' I said.

'I can't help it. S'pose he came back suddenly, without saying?'

'He won't,' said Betty. 'How d'you think he'd get from the station? Walk? Not your dad. Ring for someone to fetch him, he would.'

45

'It's me he gets crossest with,' said Edward gloomily. 'Because of being a boy.'

I said to Betty, 'Why does he get angry all the time?'

'Search me,' said Betty. 'Something wrong with his innards, I daresay.' And then, less grudging, reflective, even. 'Oh, I dunno ... He's on his own a lot, I suppose, and he's not really cut out for this kind of life. You can see that. He's a man not doing what he should in life, I'd think. He's not that fond of this place—it's not the be-all and end-all for him. That's why the war's not bothering him that much—he's not sorry for the chance to get away. But I shouldn't talk to you like this. Get off down the stables and see to the chickens.'

And we, clanking down the stable drive in the dusk, hot mash steaming up round our legs, were flabbergasted. Not that fond of Medleycott? Not that fond ... How could he? How could anyone? *Medleycott!* It was beyond comprehension.

'We couldn't have left Samba down in the stables,' said Edward. 'Not for the duration. That would have been wrong. More wrong. You have to choose, when it's two wrongs.'

And I, who had never even considered that there might be a choice, thought Good that father's gone back to Scotland and Good that Scotland's miles and miles away and please God may he not have leave again for ages and ages. And then I felt guilty for thinking it.

Edward falls on the drive. When he gets up there is a bloody patch on his knee, encrusted with gravel. He limps to the kitchen, trying not to cry, and Betty, busy with potatoes and washing, breaks off to clean the knee and prise out gravel and Edward, all restraint gone, weeps copiously.

'Be brave,' says Betty. 'Soldiers don't cry.'

Edward snarls, 'I'm not a soldier, am I?'

'No need to be cheeky,' says Betty, but she lets him have yards of bandage and he limps about with his hugely turbanned knee and everyone is sympathetic.

'Been in the wars, have you?' says Susie, and Pam, and Sandy, and Mike. I am left out, and jealous.

We knit balaclava helmets in gritty khaki wool that burns our fingers. For a few days we are overtaken with a fervour for knitting; we cannot stop—we knit at meals and in bed and sitting on the stable-yard gate. Mine is better than Edward's. Edward's leaks stitches and has airy ladders here and there and the edges are dismally crooked. We think passionately of the unseen soldiers for whom we are knitting and picture them, slit-eyed in arctic gales, stamping through the snow.

'But the war's mostly in hot places,' says Edward, puzzled. 'Africa and Malaya and out there.'

And then all of a sudden we are fed up with knitting and Betty has to finish it, sarcastic, and says, 'So that's your war effort, is it?' We feel guilty and inadequate.

A cow calves in the night, down by the stream. There is a glistening afterbirth in the grass, shrinking in the sun like a stranded jellyfish. We study it, poke it with a stick, and puzzle over it. How? Why? The rice pudding for supper has the same translucence and we refuse it with a shudder.

'One thing about the country,' said Mike. 'It does get rather spectacular at about this time of year. Now that, I will admit, you don't find in the Harrow Road.'

The hedgerows had become gardens. They had sprung into flower and we walked up from Roadwater between cliffs of stitchwort and red campion and bluebells and periwinkle and wild strawberry and yellow archangel. The colours drifted against the green—blue and pink and yellow and sparkling white. And every tree sang, every tree and bush and telephone wire. Warblers and yellow-hammers and robins and chaffinches. The landscape seemed to shout.

'Compensates a bit for muck-spreading in the ten-acre. And chopping mangels and ditching in February and threshing and mucking out and one or two other things I could mention,' said Mike.

We had met, coming up from the village, Mike wheeling his bike up the long steep bit before the plunge down into the Medleycott valley, us tramping home after doing Betty's shopping for her. We bickered about whose turn it was to carry the basket, fifty paces each, to be counted by the non-carrier.

'What's the Harrow Road?' said Edward.

'The Harrow Road? The Harrow Road, my son, is the centre of the civilized world. The Harrow Road is the gateway to all that's bright and beautiful and to be desired. The Harrow Road is where you get the bus to the Albert Hall and the National Gallery and the Tate and Lyons' at Marble Arch and Uncle Jim's and everywhere that makes life worth living.'

'Don't you like Medleycott?' we said, shocked.

'What a pair you are for taking things personally. It's just I'm used to being somewhere else. Got it? You're used to being here. I'm used to being in Woodchester Square off the Harrow Road. Right?'

'Right,' said Edward. 'Your turn for the basket, Jane.'

'Wouldn't you like to live here when the war's over?' I said.

'Tell you what,' said Mike, 'I'll borrow your big barn every August and bring Mum and Dad and the girls and Auntie Ruth and Uncle Jim and Grandma and the lot of them. O.K.?'

We were passing the old quarry.

'Now that,' said Mike, 'is really rather nice. "Farther and farther, all the birds of Oxfordshire and Gloucestershire ..." Except that we happen to be in Somerset, but the thought's the same.'

The quarry was a green cup in the fields. Bramble and hawthorn humped down its sides into the green grassy bottom. Standing on the bank at the top of the hill we looked down into it, and beyond to the spinney and beyond that again into distances that became blue instead of green, away and away to the brown rim of Exmoor against the sky. And the warblers in the quarry competed with the chaffinches in the spinney: the whole green and growing place fluttered and sang. 'Orchids,' we said, remembering. And we abandoned Betty's basket behind the hedge and ran, slipping and skidding, down into the quarry.

The orchids grew always in one place, at the far end, in a little cul-de-sac between high cliffs of bramble. Early purple orchids, in banks, and rare green ones that we did not know the name of, and, later, bee orchids. The early purples would be out now, and there were lots, not rare and special, so we could pick some for Betty.

We whooped and dodged between the mountainous brambles. All ahead and all around there was pink bramble blossom and foaming white may. Somewhere behind and out of sight we could hear Mike whistling. He whistled something complicated that we had heard him play on the violin and up above on the as yet bare branches of an ash a blackbird lurched down and whistled back at him, a simpler version. Edward bounded ahead to the orchid place and I followed. He went round a corner and I lost him.

'Edward ... *Edward!*'

He didn't answer. When I came up to him he was all among the orchids, staring at something, gone silent.

It was a rabbit's head, lying between pinnacles of orchid where bees unconcernedly clung and fed. It had empty eye sockets but shreds of fur stuck to it still, and the rag of an ear. It was hideous, appalling. We stared at it in revulsion, unable to tear ourselves away.

And then we heard Mike, scrambling among the bushes, and we turned and fled back to him, through the bramble and hawthorn that had darkened suddenly and become canyons, huge gloomy places from which we wanted to get away.

'Where are these orchids of yours, then?' said Mike amiably.

And Edward said, 'There aren't any. We've got to go back now.' And pelted away up to the lane, with Mike following, not knowing what had happened. The quarry was blasted for us now by what it held. We were ashamed of it, as though it were our fault. We didn't want Mike to know, not ever.

The rabbit's head became my private symbol of horror. For years it haunted my dreams. Now, it comes back to me in other forms: a newspaper photograph of distant wars, a crumpled car beside a motorway.

And we never went into the quarry again.

───────────────────────────────

5

Spring; summer; autumn; winter. Years are orderly things. One should be able to twitch away months from the mind, like sheets from a calendar, and say, 'Ah, yes, of course—before that happened there was this ...' But it is not so at all. In the head, all springs are one spring—a single time when we are in a garden jungly with bird-song, blackbirds sweeping across the lawn with vampire shrieks, primeval croaks and moanings in the elms. And all autumns are one purple-fingered blackberry picking and all winters are one scramble across glass-cold lino to dress quick without washing before Betty sees and down into the warm kitchen for breakfast.

And all summers are one hay-making and raspberry-time and lanes tented over with leaves and the tipping hillsides bleached pale where they have cut the corn.

On the lawn, our bike wheels have left dark ribbons on the dew. Now we stand at the top and our shadows slope down, enormous, reaching right down the grass to the ha-ha at the bottom. We jig up and down and the shadows caper with us, brushing over the buddleia and the fuschia bushes, reaching half-way up the cedar. We run, trailing them behind us, and there are four of us, zig-zagging to and fro. We climb on the gate and stare up over Croydon fields all filmy with mist, the trees waist-deep in it, floating ... It is going to be a nice day: we will ask Betty for a picnic.

Mike had a birthday, his twenty-first. Betty gave him a pullover, hand-knitted. Pam and Susie, a wallet. Sandy, forty cigarettes.

And we painted him a picture, huge, a combined effort. It was a picture of harvesting, with everybody in it—the land-girls and Mr Pitt and David and Tom Fletcher and us and Mike himself.

He pinned it on the wall of his room. 'What's the aeroplane in the corner?'

'It's one of ours. A Spitfire. Edward didn't want it in but I said it ought to be.'

'Mmm,' said Mike. 'Proper little realist, aren't you. I like it very much—thank you. Thanks very much.' And he added, 'It's my best present.' We glowed.

He didn't tell us about the cinema until the evening. They had known, all of them, and they had gone about the day in that ordinary, unconcerned way that grown-ups could manage even when something remarkable, something enormous and never-to-be-forgotten was impending ...

We were going to the cinema in Minehead. We were going to the Gaumont to see *Road to Rio*. Pam and Susie and Betty and Mike and Tom Fletcher and us. In the farm van, we were going, using petrol saved-up for emergencies. Tom and Betty had got their heads together, it

53

seemed, and reckoned we hadn't had much in the way of emergencies last winter, one way and another, and there was a bit put by, and we could all do with a treat.

We had only been once before to the cinema, and it faded into obscurity, a vague impression of tip-up seats and swishing curtains and ice-cream. This time, we lived each moment with intensity, from getting ready, having tea, getting in the van, going there, Withycombe, Carhampton, Dunster Castle ... Please God, I thought, make it go slowly this evening, last for days and days, not be ordinary time at all.

And, in a way, it did. I have it still. The queue for seats, behind a board that says Circle 1/9 (best seats for us—Mike is treating everyone); the rub of velvet on my bare legs; the thrill of dimming lights; the organ that swims up from the floor already playing; the swirl of those breathtaking rainbow-shimmering curtains. And then that warm, companionable darkness from which we plunge by proxy into the garish fairyland of Bob Hope and Dorothy Lamour and deafening song and brilliant, dazzling colour. We cannot follow the story at all : 'Why did he say that?' we hiss to Betty, 'Where are they going? Who's that?' And after a while we give up and just enjoy and laugh when everyone else laughs, and it does go on for days and days, or hours at least.

And the evening extended into more delights. We had fish and chips at a café near the cinema. We walked through the darkened streets among soldiers and girls. We saw American G.I.s and stared in unashamed amazement. There were no Americans yet near Medleycott so this was new to us, and interesting, and we stared without compunction. And some of them were black, negroes, and we had never seen anyone black except once on Minehead beach in a minstrel show, years ago, but not like this, in real life. So that was extraordinary, something to take home and mull over. And then the drive home, in darkness, with Tom Fletcher nearly going in the ditch because the headlights are all dimmed over for the blackout, so everything is excitement and giggling and we are thrown from side to side of the cold, straw-smelling van.

Back at Medleycott, we piled out at the kitchen door. There was instantly the sense of something wrong, something different: a rim of light round the door, Samba howling from somewhere outside and distant. From the stables.

'Oh, my God,' said Betty, who never, normally, said that. 'Tonight of all nights. Trust him to pick tonight.'

Father was back. A forty-eight hour leave, because they might be posted overseas. Forty-eight hours, and a twelve-hour journey standing up in the train from Scotland and there he was in the hall in a towering rage wanting to know where precisely everyone went larking off to these days? And, staring over Betty's shoulder at Mike, who precisely this might be, if someone would be good enough to inform him?

'You can't,' said Edward.

Never, never had we challenged father before, face to face, person to person. Prevaricated, yes. Evaded. Slid away from. Hid in the spinney from. But never challenged. Edward was scarlet; I, clenched with fury.

'You can't.' Desperately. 'He's billeted. Like Susie and Pam.'

'Easily seen to,' said father. 'A word with Palmer, that's all.'

'But *why*? What's he *done*?'

'He's a damn conchie,' said father. 'I'm not giving house-room to people like that. I just don't care for his type, that's all.'

'That's not something he's done,' said Edward, in passion. 'It's what he is. It's the kind of person he is. He can't help that.'

'That's enough cheek from you, Edward.'

'I think Mike's brave,' shouted Edward. 'I don't think he's a coward at all. Only stupid people think that.'

And father shouted back. 'I said that's enough! D'you hear?'

So that what follows is inevitable. Edward is sent to bed with no supper. I scream at father, through the closed door, after he has gone, 'I hate you! I think you're the meanest person in the world!' And he hears and I am condemned with Edward and sent also to bed. But separately, alone and raging in the spare room.

Later, Betty comes and dumps herself for a moment on the bed. 'There,' she says vaguely. 'There, now ... Here—don't let on, though, or there'll be more ructions.' And she smuggles me a biscuit under the bedclothes. I eat it, and choke, heaving dry sobs.

'I dunno,' says Betty, 'I really don't. You've got to give and take a bit, these days, that's what I think. But we know your dad, don't we?' She sighs.

*   *   *

Mike went without fuss. From him, that is. He packed his books and the best suit and moved down to Roadwater to a room over the pub. We raged and muttered.

'Look,' he said. 'It's not worth the carry-on, you know. I'd have gone soon anyway. The Min. of Ag. man says I'm probably going to be sent to a farm over by Taunton in the autumn.'

Edward said, 'That's not the point.'

'True enough,' said Mike. 'Put it down to experience. Yours and mine both.'

Edward wanted him to have the violin. Wanted with passion, like Edward always did things.

'But you've been playing it yourself, my son. Not so bad, either. In fact not at all dusty.'

'I *want* you to have it. That's what I *want*.'

'And don't think I'm not appreciative. But I can't lug a violin around, the life I'm leading these days, now can I? I don't think they'd relish it down at the Valiant Soldier, either.'

So the violin stayed, and Edward went on scraping and squeaking. More even, perhaps, than before, because of what Mike had said. And father. Father had heard him, later in that malevolent forty-eight hour leave.

'For God's sake, Edward! What kind of a cissy are you turning into?'

And Edward stared at him over the strings without saying anything, and then put the violin away until father had gone.

We saw Mike often enough while he was at the Valiant Soldier. On Sundays he came up and had Sunday dinner with us. This was Betty's idea, and afforded her a two-pronged satisfaction: it was a gesture of defiance at father, and, by implication, it reflected upon the Sunday dinner of Mrs Curry at the pub, which Mike would otherwise have eaten. It was, for her, a most agreeable arrangement.

And for us. Afterwards, we could persuade Mike to enliven the long wastes of Sunday afternoon. There were Edward's violin lessons ('You're coming on, my son, you're coming on. We'll make the Royal Academy yet.' —and Edward, stiff with effort, frowns and scowls and squeaks). There was reading aloud ('Come on,' says Mike, 'we'll get stuck into *Treasure Island*'—and we are stuck, swallowed up, immersed, till it is tea-time and dark). And there is going up on Croydon to see if there are any deer, and mushrooming in the Rodhuish fields and nutting in Langridge woods.

One Sunday we took Mike to see Tom Dixon. Betty was sending Mrs Dixon some Medleycott plums and apples.

The Dixons lived in one of the Roadwater cottages. Tom once worked at Medleycott but now he was retired. The cottage was one of the row backing on to the hill, so that they seemed to be the buttress that stopped the field beyond, and the hawthorn hedge-bank, and Mr Beaver's sheep, from all sliding down into the village street. The landscape was fended off by Tom's military display of vegetables, platoons and companies of onion and cabbage marching up the slope to the hedge, and Tom pottered among them, tweaking out intrusive blades of grass. And at the back door Mrs Dixon beamed and bloomed among her sweet peas.

Tom had left Roadwater once in his life only. Sixty-fours years in Roadwater, four in Flanders—1914 to 1918. On this visit, as on every one, he brought out his medals from the dresser drawer for Edward to hold. The ribbons were frayed and the metal tarnished. There was a figure with wings on one side—an angel, was it?—and on the other, words. 'The great war for civilization,' they said.

Edward said, 'What does that mean?'

'It means there weren't to be any others,' said Tom. 'That was to be the end of it. Looks like someone slipped up somewhere, eh?' and he chuckled, and looked across at Mike to share the joke, man to man. But Mike was looking at the medals, and the coronation mugs on the dresser, and the photo of Tom Dixon in his uniform.

'Not called up, young fellow?' says Tom Dixon to Mike, and Mike, hating it, we see, mutters that he is a C.O. He mutters it too quiet so that Tom, who is hard of hearing, has to ask him to say it again.

'C.O.?' says Tom. 'Conchie?' He has a swig of his tea, and we freeze, because we think he will surely feel like Sandy does about conchies, but he doesn't know Mike like Sandy does, so he won't know that Mike's a nice enough lad, when all's said and done.

'Conchie ...' says Tom again. And then he says, 'Maybe they're the only lot that got their heads screwed on right.' He clinks the medals in his hand, and says, 'They give us all one or two of these. To say thanks very much, I suppose. You can be off home now, and thanks for coming.' He laughs. 'Whoam ...' he says, 'be off whoam ...' and he swings the medals on their ribbons and dumps them back in the drawer.

'What was it like, being a soldier?' says Edward.

'It were bloody awful, son,' says Tom. And Mrs Dixon tuts and shakes her head, because you do not talk like that in company, no matter how awful, and she gives us biscuits from the Coronation tin on the shelf and we go away up the lane, eating them slowly to make them last.

Tom Dixon died towards the end of the war. Groundsel and couch grass took over the vegetable garden and when we went to see Mrs Dixon she was quenched, all the glow gone out of her. She called us 'dear' and gave us a biscuit, but she did not really want us any more. She had gone old. Old and tired. Presently she went to live with her daughter in Minehead. The cottage, thirty years later, is still there, but weekenders have it now, with a Jaguar at the gate and bathroom tacked on at the back where Tom's cabbages used to march in spring.

And so Mike was gone, and yet not gone, and for a while things went on not so very differently, except that there was a shift, a slide, in the way we felt about father. Or at least in the way I felt. Edward never talked about him, and for other people fathers seemed to be a different matter altogether. Between David and his father there was a to-and-fro even after David had been told off. Even in mutual hostility they glared at each other out of the same blue eyes and from under the same growth of pale hair.

'My dad isn't half mad with me,' David would say complacently, but that night, you knew, they would milk the cows together, and no nonsense.

'Do you ever not like your dad?' I asked David. 'Really not like?' and David stares. ''Course,' he says, but he doesn't know what I am on about, and I know he doesn't know.

The letter from Aunt Helen arrived on a Monday. I know it was a Monday because all morning we attributed Betty's bad temper to the steam and the heavy washing baskets that made all Mondays dangerous and volcanic days, to be treated gingerly. And then there were low-voiced conversations with Pam and Susie and sudden silences when we came into the kitchen, and we knew there must be more to it than that.

Aunt Helen was father's sister and the mother of our cousins, Clarice and Ian. Once or twice a year, Aunt Helen and the cousins visited Medleycott. We did not like the cousins. The occasions when they came are melted, now, into one. Clarice and I stand in the hall, mute; we eye each other, and dislike.

'You play with your cousin, now,' says Betty, and there is real threat in her voice. 'None of this going off on your own, or getting wrapped up in a book.'

A day of purgatory lies ahead. 'What do you want to play?' I say drearily, and Clarice says, 'I don't know,' and we trail round the garden and then up to the playroom.

'Do you want to play snakes and ladders?' I say, and Clarice shakes her head. She has a runny nose; it is disgusting and I dislike her even more.

Swallowdale is lying open on the sofa. I look at it longingly. If Clarice was not here that's where I would be—away on Wild Cat Island with Nancy and John and

Titty and the rest of them.

'I've read that,' says Clarice suddenly, and she fingers a book on the shelf—*Coot Club*, it is—and I see with amazement that she is longing too.

And we read. We sit either end of the old squashy sofa and read and read in silence and we come as near as we ever will to liking each other. When we hear Betty on the stairs we shut the books hastily and make playing noises until she goes away. And then we read again. It is not too bad a day, after all, and there are scones for tea.

But tolerant cohabitation for a day was quite another matter to what was proposed in Aunt Helen's letter. Outraged and disbelieving we pressed up against the comfort of the Aga and protested.

'Go and *stay* with the cousins! *Live* with them!'

'Not go to school! Have lessons with Clarice and Ian!'

'It's him not letting me know himself I can't abide,' said Betty, over our heads, to Susie and Pam. 'Just letting me know like this through her.'

Him, we knew, was father.

'Not be at Medleycott!' said Edward. And that, we realized, was the crunch. To be somewhere else. To live, wake up, go to bed, somewhere else, every day ... We were silenced by the horror of it.

'It's that offhand ...' said Betty. Pam and Susie nodded. 'As though I hadn't taken enough trouble with them. Done every mortal thing.'

And them, as we well knew, meant us. But for once these third-person references did not interest us at all. We were lost in our own spinning thoughts.

'Shame,' said Susie, 'it's a proper shame.'

And from protest we moved to bewilderment.

'*Why*? But *why*? Aunt Helen doesn't want us. Not really.'

'She doesn't even like us,' I said. Seeing, in the mind's eye, Aunt Helen's too-bright smile of greeting, feeling her too-quick goodbye kiss.

'Because your father's decided,' said Betty.

'But *why*?'

'Reasons.'

'*What* reasons?'

'One thing and another.'

We glared at Aunt Helen's letter. It lay on the table in its economy envelope. Edward was hunching his nose.

'Out of hand, you are,' said Betty, 'apparently.'

'Not compared to my brothers, they're not,' said Susie. 'He wants to see *them*.'

'Guidance, they need. Discipline,' said Betty. 'And of course she's got so much experience with children, with her own two.'

There was that in Betty's voice, an intensity beyond mere indignation, that silenced everyone for a moment. The kettle juddered and began to sing. Betty banged a pan down and poured water into it.

'I wouldn't know, of course. Not being experienced. I'll get on with the dinner, if you'll just move yourself from in front of the stove, Edward.'

'It's not personal,' said Susie.

'Isn't it?' said Betty.

I said, 'I hate Aunt Helen.' Nobody objected.

'And they need company, it seems,' said Betty. 'They're too much on their own.'

'We're not. We're at school all day.'

'That doesn't count.'

'Why not?'

'It's not your own kind.'

'Our own kind?'

'Children,' said Betty, 'that talk nice. Like your cousins.'

'Lady Muck, isn't she?' said Susie. 'Poor little blighters. Here, you can share my sandwich, I'm full up.'

Later, shaking with emotion, I stuffed Aunt Helen's letter into the incinerator. Edward watched.

'Betty'll be cross. It said train times and things.'

'I don't care.'

'It won't make any difference.'

I didn't answer.

'It won't, you know.' He went away down to the stables. Feeding the chickens, I saw his face screwed up, fighting tears.

It didn't. In Sunday clothes, Betty also, we went on the Washford train to Taunton and thence to Bristol where Aunt Helen, by equally devious routes, would meet us and the hand-over would be effected. Anguished as the departure had been, there was a certain elation about the journey. Everybody had seen us off; Pam and Susie had give us their entire month's sweet ration; Sandy had bought us comics in Minehead; we had new jerseys and socks and shoes. We were important. Like soldiers going to the front, we hung from the train windows.

Mike had come up to Medleycott specially. 'So it got

you too?' he said. 'Pretty low down trick, I call that.'

'What got us too?'

'The war, my son, the war. Victims of circumstance, like the rest of us.'

'It's Aunt Helen got us,' I said.

'Same thing, in the long run. Cause and effect. General disruption of everything. You'll be able to say you did your bit—look at it that way.'

We looked. It made no difference.

In the train, we sat crammed between Betty and strangers with shopping-baskets, string-tied suitcases, kit-bags. So interesting was the journey, so entirely different from real life, that the purpose of it became blurred and forgotten and it came as a renewed shock to find ourselves face to face with Aunt Helen under the clock at Bristol station. She kissed us too warmly and talked to Betty over our heads in a high, bright voice. Betty talked back looking not at Aunt Helen but over her right shoulder. She went and Aunt Helen led us away.

I lie in a bed that is not my bed and stare out over the neatly turned-down sheet. Leaf-shadows swarm on the curtain but they are not the shadows of Medleycott trees. A clock ticks. The hump under the bed-clothes in the other bed is Clarice, warmly sleeping. Presently I sit up and am copiously sick on to Aunt Helen's flowered chintz quilt. Clarice wakes and begins to shout.

'Only donkeys kick,' says Aunt Helen. Voice tightly reined-in, controlled. Give way a millimetre and it might soar up and away. The whole room might scream.

'She tried to trip me.' Me, scarlet, panting.

'I didn't.' Clarice, weeping.

'They called Edward a cissy.' Me, to the floor.

'He won't join in. He spoilt the game.' Ian, reasonable.

Edward just stands there. 'It doesn't matter,' he says, and I shout at him, 'It *does* matter.'

And Aunt Helen says, 'Dear God, what possessed me I don't know ...' And she bawls at us, 'Shut up, all of you, and go away!' We all stop still and stare at her because this is not how grown-ups behave, least of all Aunt Helen.

Round the dining-room table we sigh and twist our feet about the chair-legs and our pens scrape on the exercise books.

'Nice, Jane,' says Miss Hamilton. 'Much nicer writing ...' and she moves round the table to Clarice. Miss Hamilton is a wangle, Aunt Helen says, with a sweet smile, I pulled some strings and I'm not ashamed to say so. And Miss Hamilton smiles too and says oh but Mrs Wade I should have *hated* teaching in a great big school and all *sorts* of children ...

'God made the rainbow, Edward,' says Miss Hamilton kindly, her red pencil hovering, 'to show there wouldn't be another flood.'

'The sun did,' says Edward.

'God,' says Miss Hamilton smiling.

'The sun,' says Edward. 'The sun shines through the rain and the light gets bent and makes colours. It's in the natural history book.'

And Miss Hamilton says, 'It's Scripture now, dear. We

do Natural History after break.' And she writes in Edward's exercise-book, neat, with red pencil.

'I'm a dive-bomber,' says Ian. 'You be another dive-bomber, Edward. We're Messerschmitts.' He runs across the lawn, arms spread out, veering to right and left. 'Brrr ... Brrr ... Bang. Bang. Bang.' Edward follows. They run to and fro across the lawn in the sunshine, making aeroplane noises.

Edward stops. He lies on his stomach, head turned to one side. 'Come on,' says Ian. 'Come on ... Get up. I'm the R.A.F. now. I'm machine-gunning you. Come on, you've got to dodge me.'

'No,' says Edward, 'I don't want to any more.' He turns on his back and stares up into the sky.

Later Edward and I build ourselves a house behind the rubbish-heap, out of a clothes-horse and rugs. We stay there, hours, until the cousins tell Aunt Helen.

And at night, every night, Medleycott reconstructs itself inside my head and I cannot endure it. This is worse than toothache, than earache, than anything has ever been.

6 ———————————————————————

'... unfortunate,' said Aunt Helen.

'Yes.'

'... just not worked out, somehow.'

'No.'

'... all pulled our weight ...'

'Oh yes, Aunt Helen.'

'... the war.'

'Yes.'

'... your father.'

'Mmn.'

'... really the only solution ...'

And she has said it. We are going home. We are going
to Medleycott. We are going back. It is over. Medleycott.
Medleycott. Medleycott. And this is better than anything
has ever been, better than Christmas, birthdays. It isn't
possible to bear such happiness, surely we shall burst, die
of it ...

'... listening to me?'

'Oh, *yes*, Aunt Helen.'

... old enough to understand.'

'Oh, *yes*.'

'... your father can expect.'

'No, Aunt Helen.'

'... early train on Thursday.'

Thursday! Oh, Thursday! Oh, wonderful, lovely Thursday!

'Perhaps when you're older,' said Aunt Helen.

'Thank you, Aunt Helen.'

'... when the corners have rubbed off.'

'Yes, thank you, Aunt Helen. Thank you very much for having us, Aunt Helen.'

To have had it taken away and then get it back again ... It was the same—the same green-shadowed, green-of-greens drive to the house, the same red-tile kitchen smell, the same poplar-wink and pigeon-rumble and early-morning-wet-grass but a million times better, brighter, clearer. It was as though we had never seen it before. We claimed it all again in rapture, visiting everything, checking, making sure. In the earthy gloom of the potting-shed we saw that Sandy had rearranged the spades and trowels; there were onions where last year we grew carrots; the cabbages on the stable drive were huge, blue-glowing, and as we plunged among them glistening spheres of water on the leaves crumbled into wetness on our arms and legs; there was a new calf, and three new Rhode Island hens; a moorhen was nesting down by the stream.

'Eight weeks,' said Betty.

Impossible!

'To the day.'

No. A lifetime. Two.

'Look at the calendar, if you don't believe me.'

And true enough, the view of Ullswater in spring had given way to fishing-boats at Mevagissey with only Windsor Castle missing in between. And we had learned, privately, that time cheats.

'When you're unhappy,' said Edward, 'days are longer.'

And in ecstasy they slide one into another and there is no holding them.

'Bad pennies,' said Sandy. 'Just as well—I could do with a hand pulling the onions. Or four hands.'

And there were onions to be pulled and chicken-feeding and ratting with Samba in the haystack and steamy kitchen meals and away above all our own beds at night with the right disposition of sound and smell and shadow.

'What went wrong?' said Betty.

'Nothing.'

'Played her up, did you?'

'No.'

'Squabbled?'

'Jane was sick in bed,' said Edward. 'Once.'

'She'd not pack you off for that.'

'We never *said*.'

'Said what?'

'Said we wanted to go home.'

'Then what *did* you say?'

'Nothing much.'

'And her with all that experience of children,' said Betty. 'Well, well.'

'We did our lessons.'

'Edward was better at sums than Ian. Much.'

'Ah,' said Betty.

'We said thank you for having us.'

'Well,' said Betty, 'we'll have to see what we can do about guidance and all that ourselves. Inexperienced as we are. And you can go outside and clean up your gumboots for a start.'

Mike had gone. Over to a farm near Bridgwater. He wrote to us '... you carried out a successful resistance movement, I'm told. Nine out of ten for tenacity. Three out of ten for endurance. Wish I could do the same. Over here the ditches are wetter, the mangels tougher and the pig-feed heavier. Time you had a bash at a vibrato, Edward. See you sometime.'

Medleycott is clenched by frost. The hedges are a display of white and silent fireworks: the tall grasses have a frozen fall like sparklers, pale and misty they flare down at each side of the lane; each head of cow-parsley is starred and whitened; the teazles are roman candles, stiff and firm, white-whiskered. And the barbed wire—the barbed wire across the field to keep the cows off the winter wheat—the barbed wire has undergone a frost-change into something strange and wonderful, each prick spiced with a fur of small pricks, ice-white, ice-cold. We stare and stare. Barbed wire will never be the same again.

We sit on the playroom window-sill and watch the drive—the poplars and the primrose bank and the edge of the trailer and the hard outline of the incinerator. We have decided to see when day ends and night begins. The exact, the precise moment. We watch the trees blacken and the sky go harder and bluer. 'Now,' says Edward, and I say, 'No, not yet,' and we argue, and while we argue and look at the clock it has happened and the trees are not there any more but it is all one blackness and there is a yellow light wobbling in the middle of it. Sandy is going home on his bike.

On the day father came for a weekend leave I banged my head on the woodshed door. Always, one had run straight in, without stooping. Now, with sudden malevolence, the strut of wood across the top had lowered itself. And so I went to meet father at Washford with a purple lump.

'Edward been knocking you about?' said father.

'She grew an inch,' said Betty, tart, 'and forgot to reckon with it.'

Father had not come alone. There was a Major Something with him, and the Major's wife. They filled father's end of the house with laughter and the chink of glasses. Father came to the kitchen and gave crisp, brief orders to Betty. The Major's lady approached us with winning smiles in the garden but she was like someone afraid of horses, holding out the apple and dropping it before it is taken; she disliked children, as we had already known. We observed the three of them from the shrubbery, unseen, much as we observed hinds sometimes on Croydon Hill. Except that the hinds were more interesting. And more difficult to watch. We observed, too, that the Major's lady had a special voice for speaking to Betty, bright and loud. 'What a perfectly lovely apple pie, Miss

Webber. Such a treat!'

'She sounds like Aunt Helen,' I said.

'Yes.'

'Why do they do that?'

'Do what?'

'Have different voices for talking to different kinds of people?'

'Grown-ups?'

'Yes.'

'I think they can't help it,' said Edward.

'Will we?'

'Mike didn't.'

'Mike isn't grown-up,' I said. 'Nearly. But not absolutely properly.'

We practised different kinds of voices: Aunt Helen-voices and father-voices and Pam-and-Sue-voices. And Betty-to-us voices and Betty-to-father voices and father-to-Sandy voices. It was interesting and very funny. I was best at it. Edward laughed till he got hiccups. We sat on the stable yard gate and did it till we laughed ourselves into the mud at the foot of the gate and then father came. We got up.

'Ah,' said father, 'there you are.'

'Yes.'

'Not got anything to do?'

'Not really.'

'We'll be feeding the chickens in a minute,' said Edward.

'Good show.'

There was a pause. Father said, 'I gather from your Aunt Helen that you couldn't settle down at Malvern.'

Edward hiccupped. I said, 'No.'

'I take it you didn't make a nuisance of yourselves?'

'Oh, no.'

'I'm talking to you, Edward, too.'

'Yes,' said Edward. Then he said, 'It was unfortunate.' And hiccupped again.

'Are you trying to be cheeky, Edward?'

Edward went scarlet. 'No.'

I said, 'He wasn't. It's what Aunt Helen said. Unfortunate.'

'Let him speak up for himself, Jane.'

The pigeons rumbled happily on the kitchen roof.

'It's not satisfactory, this, you know,' said father.

Samba, lying in the sun, twitched one ear and went to sleep.

'Running wild like this. No education.'

'We're going to school every day,' said Edward. 'It's just that it's the holidays now.'

'It won't do,' said father.

Edward hiccupped.

'For God's sake,' said father, 'go and get a glass of water.'

We pelted up the stable drive, barging into each other, like calves let out into the field, like Samba in the morning.

And that night, in bed, Edward said, 'Does father not like me?'

'I don't know.'

'David's lucky.'

'Why?'

'His dad.'

I said, 'We've got Medleycott.'

'Yes, I know.'

Familiar shadows arranged and rearranged themselves on the curtains.

I find old photos of us in Betty's cupboard, and am astonished. Standing by the sundial in the rose garden, our heads barely came above the top of it; we were short and fat. Now, it seems to me, we are long and thin; we look down on the sundial from above, Edward a fraction more than me. And Edward's legs are not stubby and straight all the way down but thin like the saplings in the spinney, with knobs in the middle where his knees come.

We had had to re-settle ourselves at school. Nothing is static: in two months there had been changes. Relationships had thrived or faltered, three children had left and two others had come, my desk was occupied by someone else. Resentfully, I had to sit elsewhere, among the frontier desks where girls ended and boys began. It wasn't a good place. The boys flicked rubbers off the end of rulers, when Mrs Laycock was turned to the blackboard; right on the firing line, I was peppered with them and retaliated with insults and, from time to time, betrayal. Mrs Laycock liked girls better than boys.

'George Burns threw this, please.'

And George Burns, five feet tall, relief tractor-driver to his father, stands in the corner till the bell goes.

The two newcomers were brothers from Bristol, stopping with their auntie for the duration. On our first day back they cornered Edward in the playground.

'Are you with our gang, then?'

And Edward, bewildered, found himself plunged into unfamiliar arrangements of alliances and enmities. The brothers had swallowed most of the school, lock, stock and barrel; either you were with them, or you were an outcast, beyond the law, a price on your head. With difficulty, he escaped them, for that day.

In bed, that night, he said, 'I don't want to be in a gang.'

'You'll have to be. Dawn says they make all the boys.'

'David isn't.'

'You could have your own, with David.'

'I don't want to,' said Edward again. 'There's no point. It's just for being against people. I don't want to be against people. Nor does David.'

David, somehow, had managed to stay out of it. Perhaps being a head taller than the brothers, and half a stone heavier, helped. Or just that facility of his for being separate, apart, so that he always detached himself from us, at will, when he felt like it.

The next day they were waiting.

'Well then ... You on our side?'

I hung about at the playground gate.

'She your sister?'

'Yes.'

'Tell her to buzz off.'

'You'd better go on in,' said Edward unhappily.

That day he trailed on the fringes of the brothers' supporting group. Later, on the way home, he said, 'I had to.'

'What do they do?'

'They just kind of gang up on people. They took John Watkins' pencil-case and threw it in the mud.'

'What for?'

'I don't know,' said Edward. He talked in his sleep that night, shouting something at the silence.

He tried to detach himself, unobtrusively slipping apart in the playground. The brothers sent small, pliable gang members to fetch him back. With them, or at least on the edges of the group thus occupied, he threw stones at a cat, exacted tribute in the form of sandwiches from two younger boys, and blocked the bowl of the school lavatory with newspaper. On the morning of the third day, at breakfast, he said he felt ill. Betty took his temperature, said there was nothing wrong, and he went to school.

That night, he said, 'I'm going to say I don't want to be any more. Be in their gang.'

'When?'

'Tomorrow. Yes, tomorrow.'

'What do you think they'll do?'

He didn't answer.

I said, 'Perhaps they'll just leave you out of things. That's what girls would do.'

'Yes.'

He must have put it off through the morning. In the afternoon break the playground quietened suddenly at the boys' end. At our end, the skipping, hopping and aimless scurryings hither and thither continued. Presently someone said, 'They're doing something, the boys.'

'There's going to be a fight.'

'They're bashing someone up.'

After a minute, 'It's your brother, Jane Stanley.'

We went over, breaking taboos. Flailing arms and legs, stocky bodies, stern, dirty faces. Underneath them, Edward, hunched up and somehow inert. Once or twice he kicked, ineffectually.

'He's got a bleeding nose.'

'It's not fair.'

And I yelled, 'Stop it! Leave him alone!'

The brothers, and their followers, stopped for just long enough to satisfy themselves that the interruption was not serious.

'You buzz off.'

We fetched Mrs Laycock, Dawn Hosegood and I. She came out of the school-house, and the maelstrom of boys fell apart. Edward was in the middle, his nose bloody. One of the brothers, astonishingly, had a swollen and rapidly-closing eye, which instantly caught Mrs Laycock's attention.

'Who did that?'

'He did.' A chorus, indicating Edward.

'Is that true, Edward?'

'Yes,' said Edward.

'Why did you *say* you did it?' Hours, later, in the still of the spinney, where once we fled from father. After the recriminations and the punishments and the note to Betty.

'I must have. I must have kicked him.'

'But they started it.'

'I know. I said so.'

'She didn't hear,' I said. 'You should have kept *on* saying it.'

'I couldn't. She'd started taking Billy in to see to his eye.'

'But *later*. When she told you off.'

'I tried to. I kept going all red. You know ...'

'Yes. You always do.'

'She thought I was lying.'

The spinney sighed around us.

'I wish you hadn't got Mrs Laycock. Just let them go on. It'll be worse now.'

'I had to,' I said. 'You can't just let things go on. I can't anyway.'

'I wish you had,' said Edward again.

———————————————————————

As things turned out, the brothers accepted a defeat. A partial defeat, at any rate. They molested Edward, from time to time, when they remembered, when there was nothing better to do, but did not make his life the purgatory they might have done. He was allowed, like David, though to a lesser extent, to live as an outcast.

And school was only part of the day. We were anchored, always, to Medleycott. There was Medleycott, which was the centre of the world, and then there was beyond it, where you went for fun, or adventure, or because you had to. From the lane down to Washford we looked back at the roofs of Medleycott hunched among the rise and fall of the fields, and from the top of Croydon we checked the dark gathering of the Medleycott trees, and knew that everything was in its right place. The pigeons would be patrolling the drive, the goldfish cruising the canal, Sandy in the kitchen garden, Samba asleep in the dust by the back door. There was no need to see: we had it in our heads, the feel of it and the look of it and the smell of it. It reassured us in dark moments of the day, confronted by the brothers from Bristol, or incomprehensible sums, or the wrath of Mrs Laycock.

In school, Edward was best at most things. His exercise books were neatest, had the most red ticks, were shown to the School Inspectors when they came. He explained difficulties, it was found, better than Mrs Laycock. For David, he cleared up the mystery of algebra.

'The x's and y's is *pretending* to be numbers?'

'That's right.'

'You don't know what they are, like, but it's up to you to find out?'

'Yes. They're instead of, and if they're the same as each other, see, you can add them up, just like numbers.'

'Like if a cow meant three pigs, and you had two cows, you'd have six pigs?'

'Just like.'

'Why didn't she say so then?' said David.

And in the long Medleycott evenings, after chicken-feeding and tea and running Samba in the fields, he tried and tried on the violin, labouring over the handfuls of notes in the music scores Mike had left him, the enticing other-language. And he would lie on his stomach on the kitchen floor, curled against the Aga, listening to music on the wireless. If you spoke to him, he didn't hear, removed somehow in time and space. Insulated. It maddened me.

'Edward!'

'Leave him alone,' said Betty. 'You don't own him.'

'But he said he'd come to the village.'

'You go by yourself.'

'I don't like going by myself.'

'What you don't like is him doing something you don't want.'

Was that it? As grudging as that? I suppose so, in one way. Do we remember what happened, or what we think happened, or what we would like to have happened? I remember Edward doing something I didn't seem able to do in the same way, feeling left out, wanting to get him back for myself. What would Edward have remembered? A nagging voice, cutting through his own inclinations? And Betty? Children, bickering, making an obstacle in her busy day?

But mostly we were as we always had been—doing things together, disagreeing, making it up, forgetting about it, telling each other things in a kind of shorthand because there is a point at which you know another person so well that you do not always need language for communication. Like Samba and Jip could bristle to tell each other that there were rabbits at the bottom of the field.

So that it was without having spoken of it, but by agreement, that I sat next to father in the back of the van when we went to meet him at the station on his next leave.

'Everything just the same here, I suppose?'

'Yes,' I said.

'Behaving yourselves?'

'Yes.'

We turned up the Medleycott lane. Father didn't notice that the big oak on the corner had come down in a gale.

'There are three calves.'

'Really?' said father.

'We've got eighteen laying pullets.'

'That so?' He stared out of the window. 'Who's that?'

'Pam,' I said, amazed. It was like not knowing the word for a chair, or a wheel, or a tree.

'Who's she?'

'The *land-girls*.'

'Oh, yes,' said father vaguely. Then, 'What's the hot water situation nowadays? I need a bath.'

'We take it in turns. It's Susie's night.'

'Mmm. Well, Edward—you're very quiet ... What are you doing with yourself these days?'

Edward said brightly, 'All sorts of things.'

'Such as?'

'Well ... I'm doing about newts for Nature Study, at school. And I'm reading *Kidnapped*. And I can do a vibrato ...' He stopped, went scarlet.

'A what?'

'Nothing. That's all really. And helping with the chickens and things.'

'I see,' said father. He went into the house as soon as we got back, and presently we heard him running a bath.

The next morning he sent a message through Betty that he wanted to see Edward in the study.

We are in the spinney, and a cold spring wind pours through the trees. We huddle in the long grass.

'But *why*?'

'He just said I've got to.'

'When?'

'Next term,' says Edward.

'Next *term*!'

'He says he never made all this fuss about going to

83

boarding school. He says I've got to accept that I'm growing up.' There is no resentment in Edward's voice: just a bleakness.

'Had you made a fuss?'

'I said I didn't want to.'

'David's growing up too,' I say passionately. 'He's the same age as you. He hasn't got to.'

'I know,' says Edward. His nose twitches.

And I say, furiously, because I am near to tears, 'You're doing that thing with your nose again.'

'Am I? Sorry.'

Father was going overseas. Where, we were not to know, neither did we ask. And he had come home to tie up loose ends. Such as the lease of the Roadwater cottage, and the repair of the stable roof. And Edward.

Numb with disbelief, we roamed the garden and the fields and beyond, Edward white and silent, I shouting our outrage at anyone who would listen.

'Father's sending Edward to boarding school.'

'Well now, there's a turn-up for the books,' said Sandy. He looked at me, through a wigwam of runner-bean poles. 'What about you, then?'

'I can go on going to school at Washford, because I'm a girl.'

'Ah,' said Sandy. 'It's always the women that get left to keep the home fires burning.' And he lashed the poles with raffia, whistling to himself.

Whistling, when the world was coming to an end. And the pigeons went on rumbling their contentment on the roof above our heads, every day, and people could laugh with the postman outside the back door, and Pam's soldier friend waited for her in the lane, leaning against the gate-post. And Medleycott betrayed us with indifference. It should have shrivelled, mourned: instead, the daffodils blazed from one end of the garden to the other, the grass shone silver in the wind, the rooks nested, tadpoles appeared, and each bit of the place was blessed still with its own smell—balsam poplar and thyme and compost and damp spring earth.

The day father left I could hold it back no longer. Where was Edward? Goodness knows. In my head, now, there are father and I, face to face in the drive, the car waiting.

'Look,' says father, 'it happens to all of us. Edward's got to accept that. When I was at school it was a lot tougher than it is now, I can tell you.'

'How old were you?'

'How old was I when?'

'When you went to boarding school?'

'Seven.'

Seven. *Seven?*

'And it hasn't done me any harm, has it?' says father.

'Did you mind?'

'Mind what?'

'Weren't you miserable? Wanting to go home.'

'Don't be damn silly, Jane—how should I know now? Anyway, if I was I daresay I soon got over it. Edward's got to learn to face up to things a bit—life's not all a bed of roses, you know. He's got to learn that, like any other boy.'

I said, 'David's not got to. Go away.'

'David down at the farm, do you mean?'

'Yes.'

'For heaven's sake—it's different for that kind of boy.'

'Why? *Why?*'

'Good grief, Jane—I should have thought you were old enough to see that.'

And suddenly I can't go on like this.

'It's us belong here,' I wail, 'not you. I wish you'd go away and not come back. Not ever come back to Medleycott again.'

And father says, 'May I remind you that this is my house, Jane.' Coldly, as grown-up to grown-up.

'And may I remind you that Edward is my brother.' But I am hopelessly out of joint, trying his level. I sound younger, not older. Rude, not outraged. I feel foolish and humiliated. The car goes, and father with it. I am left standing among the pigeons, in front of the house.

And that night I dream of lions. They have escaped from their cage and they are coming for me, rushing down upon me ... And there is no escape, they will have me. But somehow they do not. They pass me and beyond me there is this woman and they will have her instead I see, but she is not afraid of them. She stands still and they stop and she is stroking them. They are not lions any more: they have got smaller. I wake up, crying.

There were eighteen days left, and then twelve, and then six, till Edward was to go. And then suddenly it was tomorrow, and Betty had brought the old trunk down from the attic and packed it in the playroom—

grey flannel shorts and long socks and jerseys and strange garments we have never seen before.

'What's that?'

'It's a rugger shirt.'

Edward sat on the edge of his bed, speechless, and I felt, vicariously, in my own stomach, the cold hard knotting that must be in his.

'Why's he got to have all those shoelaces?'

'Search me,' said Betty, consulting lists.

'And towels. Why can't the stupid place give them towels?'

'The war, I suppose. What books do you want to take, Edward?'

'You can have all the Arthur Ransomes,' I said. 'And *Treasure Island* and the William books and *Tales of Ancient Greece*.' I pulled books from the shelf in handfuls.

'Thanks,' said Edward.

'Come on,' said Betty. 'Let's have a smile. It won't be as bad as all that. We'll all be keeping our fingers crossed for you.'

And the last times began ... The last time feeding the chickens, the last time going down to the stream, the last time having tea in the kitchen, the last time going to bed.

And the last time going down the drive and out through the gate and along the lane between the high hedges and through Washford and up the steps on to the platform to wait for the train. I knew how Edward must be feeling and I could not bear it. I would be going back, back down the steps and up the lane and in at the Medleycott gates again; to be doing that, without him, was like stealing. It felt grubby, as though it was my fault.

'Chin up now,' said Betty, privately, under cover of the car engine. 'Don't you go getting him more miserable than he already is.'

And so all the way to the station, and waiting on the platform, and putting Edward into the train, there was brave talk about things that did not much interest anybody, words for the sake of words, and as soon as the carriage doors were slammed shut and the train oozing steam, and clanking, and then gone away down the track, I streamed tears. And streamed on, at intervals, all through the rest of the day and half the night and waking up the next morning.

I feel grey and shrivelled. I have stopped crying and walk about like someone who has been ill, long bed-ridden, with short, careful steps. My legs have gone weak. I examine myself, gingerly, and find that I am not unhappy any more. Nor happy, either. I am nothing: a person in a limbo. Who are those people the Greeks knew about—the ones who wander around the Styx? The unburied dead: grey, unpeople. I am one of them.

Edward's letters seemed to come from nowhere. He told us nothing, and wanted to know everything. 'Dear Everyone,' he began, and then he wanted to know how many eggs the new pullets were laying and if the fly-catchers had nested by the kitchen window and please could someone put the violin away where it wouldn't get dusty because he forgot. Could you, he said, send me my penknife and my postcard collection and some leaves from the sycamore on the lawn.

'Leaves?' said Betty. 'Has he gone barmy?'

But I collected the leaves, and the flat pale green keys with them, and flattened them under the *Encyclopaedia Britannica*, Vol. 1, and put them in an envelope. And wrote to Edward. To *Edward*, to whom I had never written in my life. I could think of nothing to say. Nothing at all. I sat staring at the blank page, and in the end the letter said thank you for your letter Samba is very well and the chickens and the cows here are the sycamore leaves I put the violin in the playroom cupboard Love from Jane.

Betty wrote, saying Come along now, we want to know how you're getting on, are they feeding you properly and what are the beds like?

And the answer came in the next letter, pencilled as a P.S. after a page of questions. 'It's cold,' he said. No more.

'Cold?' said Betty. 'In May?'

Day succeeded day. I went to and from Washford to school; fed the chickens; ate; slept each night beside Edward's flat, counterpaned bed; trailed with Sandy in the garden under a clamour of rooks that I seemed never to have heard before. Had they always made that noise? Standing in the drive, staring up to where they swirled above the chestnuts, it seemed something new. And up in the playroom, reading in the corner of the sofa, I discovered the loudness of the mantelpiece clock. Had it always battered the silence like that? Or had there, with two of us, never been such silence?

It was from there, on a wet Sunday, lying face-down on the black and red carpet playing patience that I heard Mike's voice on the stairs.

'Jane?'

He fought off Samba's welcome, and sprawled on the sofa. He seemed longer and thinner than ever.

'How did you *get* here?'

'You may well ask. Combination of hay-making being rained off, and someone going as far as Williton in a car, and then there actually being a bus to the cross-roads ... And now what's all this I hear?'

'Edward?'

'Precisely.'

'Father sent him to boarding school.'

Silence. Samba gazing at Mike as though she might melt. The clock yammering on. Then Mike said, 'That was a bad move. That was really a very poor move indeed.'

'He just said he'd got to.'

'He does have rather a knack of putting his foot in it, your father.'

'I think he's miserable,' I said, 'Edward.'

'If there was one person it wouldn't do to pack off like that, it would be old Edward,' said Mike. 'Poor old son.'

'He's coming home for half-term. In six weeks.' Six weeks four days.

'I see.'

'It'll be worse,' I said, 'coming back and then going again. Knowing it's just three days.'

'Could be.'

There was a long silence. 'Put the red queen on the black king,' said Mike. 'And you can get that one out. Then we'll go up on Croydon, rain or no rain. Right?'

We sat on the gate-post at the top of the hill. Fields and hedges, brilliant after the rain, ranged neatly away to the coast and the white gleam of the Bristol Channel. Down in Rodhuish, a mile away, the farm dogs barked and we could have reached out and touched the sound. There were threads of smoke from houses in Watchet and on the horizon the long misty coastline of Wales.

'If this was Dover,' said Mike, 'that would be France.'

'There'd be Germans there.'

'Just so. Not quite so comfortable to look at.'

Mike lit himself a cigarette. 'Looks better from up here than when you're down there in the middle of it heaving machinery around.'

'Do you still want to go back to the Harrow Road?'

'You bet I do.'

Offended on behalf of west Somerset I was silent.

'Insensitive brute, aren't I?' said Mike.

'No.'

'Just a bit?'

'Well—it's the same as us not wanting to go away from Medleycott, I s'pose.'

Mike laughed. 'You s'pose ... But you're bothered if you can see why, that it? Here ...'

'Gosh—thanks. But it's your ration.'

'I've gone off toffees. Toffees and muck-spreaders and getting up at five o'clock. And being The Conchie.'

'Aren't they nice—where you are now?'

'Not bad, I suppose. They come in all shapes, like

91

people usually do. And I get a good chance to be on my own. I've got a barn all to myself.'

'A barn!'

'Hayloft really. They've set it up as a place for me. Not half bad. Bed, room for all my stuff, and the pigeons for company. And nobody coming up to see what I'm up to.'

We went home and had tea. Mike had to go. Before he went, down at the stables, he got a pencil out and wrote on the back of an envelope.

'Here—the next time you're wanting someone to complain to. You or Edward.'

'I'll lose it,' I said helplessly.

'Useless child,' said Mike. He licked the end of the pencil and wrote on the white-washed pillar of the stable 'Acre End Farm, Chedzoy. Telephone Chedzoy 47.' 'There. Just don't let them clean the wall for a year or two.'

'Will you come again?'

'You never know.'

8

I don't know how, now, but the six weeks four days went by. They went, and it was June, and Edward came off the Washford train, in grey shorts and a blazer.

'Go on,' said Betty, 'give him a kiss.

We ignored her, and stared at each other.

'You've had your hair cut.'

'We've all had to.'

'What's that? The envelope thing.'

'It's the emergency ration card. For Betty. Can we go?'

At Medleycott, he seemed in a daze.

'You sort of can't believe it.'

'Believe what?'

'Believe it's real. Believe you're really back. It's like dreaming. You might wake up.'

'You won't,' I said. And we went mad, suddenly. We roared from one end of the drive to the other on our bikes, skidding round the corner, screaming; we stood in the middle of the lawn and spun, arms out, till we fell with dizziness and lay on grass that turned and whirled; we climbed the Cedar of Lebanon and the quince and the chestnut by the stables; we sang.

There were spam fritters for supper, and scrambled

egg, and apple with real crumble on top, as much as we liked.

In bed, that night, across the three foot gap of lino and the old rag mat with a cat's face picked out in red, I said, 'What time do you have to go to bed there?'

'Don't. Don't talk about it. Not now.'

'Is it awful?'

'Yes.'

'As bad as Aunt Helen's?'

'Much, much worse. Not like that at all. Ssh.'

'Goodnight.'

'Goodnight.'

There had been a letter from father. He expected, he said, that Edward had settled down at school by now and he was sorry not to be able to get to Medleycott to see us. He'd wanted to hear how the cricket was going, he said. But the fact was that he had at last got his overseas posting and would be off in about a week's time, and there were one or two things he had to see to in London so he was taking his embarkation leave there.

'Where's he going?' we asked, over breakfast.

'Can't say that, can he? Don't know themselves, do they, half the time?'

'Far East, it'll be,' said Pam.

'Miss Know-all, as usual. North Africa, more like.'

'Look, it's all the Far East now, isn't it? You've only got to listen to the news. Stands to reason ...'

'When will he come back?' said Edward.

They look at each other, the grown-ups.

'Quite a long time it'll be, I should think, love,' said

94

Susie. 'All that way. They don't get home leaves much, out there.'

'Months? A year?'

'You can't say,' said Betty. 'Of course he'd have got down if he could, I daresay.'

'I don't mind. I just wondered, that's all.'

'Can we go?' I said.

Outside, tugging our boots on, we could hear them talking still.

'Mind you, he's never had a lot to do with them, when all's said and done ...'

'He should have come down, if you ask me ...'

'Top up the pot, there's a dear.'

'Come *on*,' said Edward. 'We've got to go down to Escott. And to Roadwater and up on the hill and to see David and everything. Come *on*.'

We had two days. Two days and a half day but the half day didn't count because of what would happen at the end of it. Two days and you mustn't think beyond the two days because that would spoil everything, you might as well not have them. So we didn't think. The moments when we saw the clock, or suddenly it was tea-time when surely dinner had only just been, we pushed way from us, retreated from. If you can't see it, it won't hurt you; if you pretend it isn't happening, it will go away.

Only Edward, at moments, coming up the lane from David's, sprawling in the sun by the lavender hedge, polishing the violin, went silent and stricken.

The last day, the half-day, he got up silent. I couldn't bear it.

'What are you *thinking* about?'

'Nothing.'

I knew, though. Six hours till the train. Five and a half. Five.

We migrated from one part of the garden to another, aimlessly. In the iris garden, we sat by the canal and stared at the water boatmen and the tadpoles. Edward snapped the heads off daisies and dropped them into the water.

'The goldfish won't eat them.'

'I know.'

'Why are you doing it, then?'

'Just for something to do,' said Edward.

'We could go down to the stream.'

'It's not worth it.'

I said, 'I hate father. Don't you?'

He didn't answer, squashing the yellow centres of daisies between his fingers.

'Don't you? Edward ... Don't you?'

He blinked, mangling flowers.

'You *ought* to.'

'No.'

'*Yes.*'

'I don't want to,' he said. 'It's school I hate, not him.'

'But it's him who's ...'

'I know. But you don't think about that, when you're there. It's just *it*—being there.'

'Does everybody hate it?'

'No. Lots of them like it. There's a boy who cries every night. You can hear him, on and on. You can't say so—that you're miserable—or they call you a cissy.'

I couldn't find anything to say.

96

'What's worst is when I dream sometimes I'm here, and then when I wake up I'm not.'

We sat there in the sun. I looked at him, and appallingly, horrifyingly, he was crying. His face stayed smooth but his eyes seemed to swell and the tears slid down and made dark spots on his grey flannel trousers.

'Oh, don't ... Please don't.'

He wiped his hand across his face. And then he said in an ordinary, flat voice, 'I'm not going back. I can't.'

'They'll make you. Betty ...'

'I've thought,' he said, 'I've thought all night. I'm going away till father's gone overseas. I'll hide somewhere. Then I'll come back. When he's gone Betty wouldn't send me back.'

He meant it. It was desperate, and it couldn't work. But it might. It just might. She just might not.

'We haven't got any money.'

'We have. There's my birthday money still, and this term's pocket money. I looked before breakfast. It's one pound five and six.'

'Where will you go?'

'I ... I'm not sure.'

I said, 'I'm coming too. And I know where we'll go.'

Is it because I don't want to that I can't remember what happened next? Because of the guilt? Because of knowing that you can't do something like that to people you love, people who love you? To Betty and the rest of them. Probably. We are in the iris garden, and then, somehow, we are walking up the Medleycott drive, with all the money we have, and some apples in our pockets, and an address in our heads, 'Acre End Farm, Chedzoy'. And at the top of the lane, when it is still not too late, Edward looks at me and says, 'I've got to. I can't go back there.' And I say, 'I know.'

We didn't stay in the lane. Once the point of no return was reached, the point when it was real, actually happening, we went into the fields and walked from field to field, through hedges and over gates that we knew almost as well as the Medleycott garden.

'How far is it?' said Edward.

'I'm not sure. Further than Bridgwater.'

'That's twenty miles. More than twenty miles, then.'

And for the first time it occurred to us that we weren't going to get there that day. It would get dark, and we would have to sleep somewhere. We would have to sleep somewhere, in our clothes, without pyjamas or tooth-brushes. Guilt stalked beside us, among the thistles and the cowpats and the stands of nettles.

'What time is it?'

'Half-past one.'

'They'll be having dinner.'

'No,' said Edward. 'They'll have started looking for us.'

After a moment he said, 'Do you want to go back?'

'Do you?'

'I can't. Not go back to school. I just can't.'

'Then I'm not going back.'

That was the point at which we could still choose. We could have turned round and gone back and we would have been late for dinner. No more than that. I don't know, now, how we slid over that moment and into the situation, only half real, as though perhaps we were dreaming, where we were really doing it. Where there was no going back.

It was probably because we got lost. We climbed over a gate and out into the lane that would take us down towards Williton, but it didn't. It went up instead and wound endlessly between arching hedges and we went on and on and presently our legs were beginning to ache and we were thirsty and Edward's watch had stopped. That was the final chop from reality, the watch stopping. If we didn't know what time it was we couldn't think of what they might be doing and so we couldn't think of them. They weren't there any more: there was just us.

'I'm terribly thirsty,' said Edward.

'How far have we gone?'

'Miles.'

'Do you think we're nearly there?'

And it came to us that we didn't at all know where we were, which way we should go, where Chedzoy was.

'Are we lost?' I said.

'I s'pose so.'

But it didn't feel very lost, sitting on a bank at the edge of the lane in all respects like one of the Medleycott lanes, except that it wasn't. The hedge was furnished with the same toadflax and red campion and bramble sprays; the same yellowhammer sang on a telegraph wire just ahead; the same butterflies flickered above the grass. A man trudged past wheeling a bike, glanced at us, and said, 'Afternoon,' in the voice of Sandy, or David's dad, or Tom Fletcher. Lost implied outlandish, not familiar.

'Afternoon,' we said, and when he was out of sight round the bend we got up and followed him. He must be going somewhere.

At the next crossroads there was a scatter of cottages, and a stream, from which we drank.

'There's a shop.'

'Let's buy something for tea.'

There wasn't much we could buy. Bread. Some Oxo cubes to chew. The lady in the shop asked where we came from, and we went away quickly, mumbling too low for her to hear. For the first time we remembered that in other places as well as in Rodhuish and Roadwater everybody knows everybody else. We, too, stared at strangers; never before had we been the strangers.

Disconcerted, we ate the bread out of sight of the houses, in a field.

'We've got to ask someone the way. We might be going in the wrong direction.'

'We can't. They'll ask things back.'

'We'll find children,' said Edward.

We went back to the crossroads. There was a boy of five or six by the stream, who could only say, 'I dunno'.

'Is it that way to Bridgwater? Or that way?'

'I dunno.'

A girl came, our age, and started dragging him away. 'Mum says you come along in.'

'Which way is it to Bridgwater?'

'The bus has gone.'

'I know,' said Edward. 'Is it that way, though?'

She nodded.

'Is there another bus?' I said.

' 'Course not.' They went away, turning to stare at us once or twice.

'Come on,' said Edward.

The lane climbed around the edges of hills, went steeply up, plunged down into valleys, forked, twisted. We met no one. We had to keep stopping to rest.

Edward said once, 'It'll be all right when we get there.'

We walked until our legs hurt too much to go on, and then we stopped and sat disconsolate on banks or beside haystacks. Then we got up and went on, then we stopped again. So on for days, not hours; leagues, not miles. Once or twice, incredibly, we seem to have forgotten where we were, or why, or what we were doing. We squatted once, I know, beside an enthralling stream where minnows flicked over pebbles and in the deeper parts bigger fish plopped from time to time.

'Trout,' said Edward.

'In *Swallows and Amazons* they eat them. They make a fire.'

'You'd have to kill them first.'

'How?'

'Bang their heads?' said Edward doubtfully.

And all of a sudden the image of the rabbit in the quarry swam before us, shared but unmentioned, and we left the trout where they were.

We passed cottages, and an occasional farm. Once we checked the direction with a boy swinging on a gate.

'How many miles is it to Bridgwater?' said Edward, offhand.

'Why d'you want to know, then?'

'Just wondered.'

'Why are you walking to Bridgwater?' said the boy.

'We aren't,' I said. 'We just wondered.'

After that, we didn't talk to people. Not even children.

And then it began to get dark. First we didn't notice. It was as though, just, the sun had gone in for a bit. And then everything was thickening around us and trees and hedges were only inadequately there and in the over-hung bits of the lane we stumbled on stones we hadn't seen. Now we knew, and pretended not to.

'It takes ages, getting dark,' said Edward.

But it doesn't. We should have known. Once, we had sat at the playroom window at Medleycott and tried to pin down the moment when it is night, and it had cheated us, got past us.

I said, in panic, 'We can't sleep outside.'

'Gypsies do. Tramps.'

'I don't want to.'

'Neither do I,' said Edward.

Darkness comes, every day, and you accept it. You draw the curtains, take a torch, switch the light on: it is temporary and natural. That darkness was not. It was terrifying, as though happening for the first time, at the Creation. It was total, unstoppable, and everybody else in the world except us was inside a house.

'We could knock on somebody's door.'

'Ask if we could stay there?'

'Yes,' I said. Knowing that you could not.

'Not people we don't know,' said Edward. It was true. To do something that one simply did not do was more impossible than to spend the night outside, unhoused.

We could no more have done it than we could have asked a stranger to give us money.

'Anyway, they'd ask why we were there.'

'Anyway, there aren't any houses.' I began to cry: privately, at first, then aloud, sniffing and hiccupping.

'Sorry,' said Edward hopelessly.

And then, round the next twist in the lane there was, suddenly, a house. At least not a house but a cottage, and not a cottage but half a cottage because against the violet sky was the black laddering of a slateless, thatchless roof, and one wall was half-crumbling, with an iron grate lurching from it, and saplings fingering up through the plaster.

We went in through the gaping door, holding on to each other. Inside there were heaped leaves, piles of rubble, and a blackbird that shrieked out through the glassless window. It was a horrid place.

We huddled among leaves and a sack in one corner, where there was some roof left intact. The night blackened around us until we could no longer see the squares of the windows, and among the leaves there were crawlings and rustlings, indefinite and dreadful. We twitched and shifted and fidgeted. We must, too, have slept.

'Do you think it's nearly morning?'

'I don't know.'

But it couldn't have been. The black hours inched on. Were nights really as long as this? I thought of days, that so much is crammed into—getting up, and morning, and dinner, and afternoon, and tea, and evening—and knew that they must be.

'I'm cold.'

'So am I.'

'It's my fault,' said Edward. 'I should have gone by myself.'

'You didn't know where to go.'

'No.'

Hours later, again awake, I said, 'We weren't there to feed the chickens.'

'Pam or Susie would do it.'

'I expect so.'

And that much, only, of Medleycott, did we allow to intrude. The rest we somehow shut off. Except that once Edward said, whispering for some reason, his breath hot and damp on my neck, 'I'll explain to Betty why I had to. She will understand, won't she?'

'Oh, yes,' I said.

And at a point when the night was blackest and longest we must have fallen asleep, clobbered, pole-axed. And slept and slept.

We woke to bird-clamour, bright light, and aches in our arms and legs. And a grey and shabby rush of guilt and desolation, worse even than the night itself. We were dirty, too, and damp, and gripingly hungry.

Edward looked awful. White, with grey hollows under his eyes, and dirt and dead leaves all over him. We picked bits off each other as we walked down the lane, and when we came to a cattle trough we washed ourselves. Things felt a bit better.

'It must be quite late,' said Edward. 'Those cows have been milked.'

We thought of milk.

'We'll have to get something to eat.'

We arrived, at last, in a village. The shop, again, offered little that you could buy without a ration book. We got some bread, a jar of fish-paste, some broken biscuits that were off points, and more Oxo cubes. In a gateway, ravenous, we ate in silence.

'I know where we are now,' said Edward. 'It's called West Quantoxhead. There was a pile of parcels in the Post Office, all addressed to it.'

He seemed less defeated, suddenly.

'How far is it from where we're going?'

'I don't know. Anyway we've got to go through Bridgwater first.'

'A long way, though?'

'I don't know,' he said patiently.

We sat, unable to make decisions. And then, reliable and familiar, there came a green bus. Round the corner it came, past us, and sat, benignly throbbing at the stop a few yards away that we had not even noticed. The back of it said 'Bridgwater'.

'Come on.'

We got on. Edward paid the fares. The conductor was a woman.

'Two halves to Bridgwater? Return?'

'What?'

'Return. Are you coming back, dear.'

'No, thank you.'

'Two singles. No school today, then?'

'It's half-term,' said Edward. And went scarlet, the colour sweeping his face.

When the conductress had gone I said, 'It is, sort of.'

'No,' said Edward, 'not today. Only up to lunch-time yesterday.' He was plunged in wretchedness again. We sat in silence all the way to Bridgwater.

Getting out of the bus in the town we had no idea what to do next. The unfamiliar place reached away all around us. Shops, people, bicycles, buildings. The country-side, in which, somewhere, was Chedzoy, Acre End Farm, Mike (and, but we did not allow ourselves to think of that, Medleycott) was invisible and we did not know how to get back to it. We trailed around streets, aimlessly, for ages. And, like yesterday, the present became occasionally so absorbing that we forgot what brought us here, what we were caught up in.

'There's a cinema.'

We gazed at it, hungrily. It had coloured photographs in frames outside, and we studied them as avidly as comics. It seemed amazing that there was no charge for this; we worked our way, three times, through them. People in what we recognized as historical costumes romped about on horseback, swarmed the rigging of ships, fought each other, embraced. It was lovely.

I said, 'We could go.'

'Go in? See it?'

'Yes.'

We stared at the cavernous, inviting jaw of the cinema. People went in, bought tickets, passed into an inner darkness from which came gusts of music. It was easy. We could too. There was nothing to stop us.

'We shouldn't,' said Edward.

But we shouldn't be there at all, in Bridgwater, alone.

That being the case, the rules of real life hardly seemed to apply. It was like, in dreams, all barriers are down: you can be naked, say outrageous things. And yet, last night, we could not possibly have knocked on the door of a strange house.

'We shouldn't,' said Edward again.

And we went in.

There was darkness, and thunderous noise. We stumbled over feet and legs to empty seats, and gave ourselves up to it. Like sleep, it was—all emotion gone, all involvement with the world, all bother, all weeping and gnashing of teeth. Cushioned in red plush, battered by gunfire and huge, distorted voices, disembodied, we abandoned ourselves to it. It was like being happy.

——————————————

9

Coming back to real life was appropriately drab, like
waking up that morning all over again. The lights went
up; there were cigarette stubs and mess on the floor; a
smell of sweat and people; my feet had gone to sleep
and my head ached; Edward said he felt sick.

We stood blinking in the street, adjusting ourselves.
What we had just done seemed suddenly preposterous,
ludicrously rash, pointless. In my head I seemed to hear
Betty's voice ... 'You went to the *cinema*? You mean
to tell me, in the middle of all that, you just went to the
cinema ...'

'Wasn't it good?' said Edward glumly.

'Lovely.'

The clock above the jeweller's shop opposite said five-
past three.

'It's afternoon,' said Edward, horrified.

Afternoon. And afternoon would be followed by evening which would be followed, as we now so unpleasantly
knew, by night.

'We've got to get to Mike.'

How? Which way? How far?

'We'll have to ask people.'

'Ask that lady,' said Edward. 'She looks nice. The one with the shopping-basket.'

'No, you. You're the oldest.'

'Bags not.'

And, shamefully, we were squabbling. Tired, cross, longing to be anywhere but where we were. Edward gave in, suddenly, and went over to her.

'She says it's that road, but quite a long way. A few miles.'

The woman was staring at us, puzzled.

'We'd better go,' said Edward. 'She started asking things.'

We walked.

'She said there's a bus sometimes. But she didn't know when.'

The buses, though, were all destined elsewhere. 'Taunton', they said, or 'Minehead', or 'Bristol'. We walked, on pavements that made our feet hurt, past shops, and rows of houses that seemed endless. The world was not, as we had thought, made up of fields, woods and lanes, but of tarmac, brick and lamp-posts. Lack of food and sleep made us feel at once detached and leaden. Our feet dragged and our heads floated. We went into a steamy café and bought sandwiches and a nameless soup, which made us feel better.

And at last the houses trickled away into fields. Flat, marshy fields, not like our own tipping, lumpy land-scape. For the first time we felt a sense of travel: we had gone, somehow, off the map.

Edward was obsessed now by time.

'I should have put my watch right, when we saw that

clock. What time do you think it is?'

It could have been anything. I had no idea. The sky was white and sunless.

'D'you think it's getting dark?' said Edward. He stared at the hedges, as though darkness lurked behind them, about to swarm over.

'Please don't go so fast.'

'We've got to.'

I trailed behind. His grey-shorted forlorn figure was ten yards ahead, then twenty. At corners he would stop for me to catch up.

'Please hurry.'

'I'm trying.'

The flare of energy that had allowed us to squabble in Bridgwater had died away now. When my legs and feet protested so that I could go no further Edward sat in silent resignation while I lay in the entrance to a gate. A tractor passed us, pulling a trailer. When we moved on we found it halted round the next bend in the lane, its driver tinkering with the engine.

Edward slowed up, and eventually stopped.

'Is it far to Chedzoy?'

'Eh?'

'Is it much further to Chedzoy?'

'Tidy bit.'

He must have seen the despair on our faces, this man.

'Got to get over there?'

'Yes.'

'Get on in, then.'

It was like a divine intervention. And no questioning, either. We scrambled into the trailer and sat among wisps of straw and crumbs of dried manure. The tractor engine roared into life again and killed any possibility of conversation. We rocked onwards between the hedges, aching, relieved, and suddenly quite passive. I thought of nothing at all. It would have been quite acceptable to go on like this for ever.

At last the tractor stopped. The man was shouting something above the roar of the engine.

'Where's it you're wanting, then, I said?'

'Acre End Farm.'

He pointed. 'End of the lane. Yard on the right.'

'Thank you *very* much,' we said, best-manners voices over the manure and the engine. He nodded.

'Cheerio.'

'Cheerio.'

We started up this lane. And for Edward, I saw, consternation had set in.

'Suppose,' he said, 'he isn't pleased?'

'Mike?'

'Yes.'

'He likes us,' I said. 'Doesn't he?'

'I know. All the same.'

'He said next time you're wanting someone to complain to . . . That's why he wrote the address on the wall.'

'He meant write a letter,' said Edward unhappily.

'It'll be all right. Honestly.'

'Suppose he just said no sorry you'll have to go back.'

'He won't,' I said, no longer certain.

A farmyard opened off the lane to the right. A farmyard like any other farmyard. Mud; sacks of feed; chickens; a cat squatting at the foot of a wall; rusting hunks of farm machinery. From beyond the open doors of a barn came the shufflings and breathings of cows.

We hesitated, suddenly quite stricken and appalled with the enormity of what we had done. Of what we were doing. I closed my eyes and wished, with intensity and passion, that I might open them and find myself transported back, quite simply, just like that, to Medleycott. 'Please God,' I said, silently. 'Make me be in the kitchen at Medleycott.'

I opened my eyes again, and I wasn't. And at that moment Mike stepped out of the barn.

He saw us at once.

'Well! Surprise, surprise. Fancy seeing you.'

We stood there.

'Come in and meet Mrs Cheadle,' said Mike. 'I daresay she'd run to some tea. Who brought you, then? Tom?' He looked beyond us, at the gateway.

There was nothing to say, suddenly.

'Betty? Betty with you, is she?'

An aeroplane pottered across the bit of sky just above the barn roof.

'She's at Medleycott,' said Edward.

'Look,' said Mike, 'what is all this?'

The aeroplane got to the end of the barn and went behind some trees. I had to stop looking at it and look at Mike instead. We stood there, staring at each other.

Mike said, 'Am I getting this right? There isn't anybody with you?'

We stood. At last Edward said, 'No.'

'You've come here all by yourselves?'

'Yes.'

'How?' said Mike.

'We walked, mostly,' I said.

Mike was looking at Edward. 'Did you,' he said, 'have to go back to school?'

Edward nodded.

'Oh, Lord,' said Mike, 'I might have guessed it.'

'You said,' I said, 'next time you're wanting someone to complain to ...'

'Yes, I did, didn't I?' said Mike. 'Yes, I see.' He was still looking at Edward. And then he said, 'You walked, mostly. You mostly walked from Medleycott. That's more than twenty miles. That was yesterday, then?'

'Yes.'

'Oh, my God,' said Mike, 'just hang on a minute. Phone call to make before we go any further.'

He walked over and into the farmhouse. Another aeroplane began its crawl along the barn roof.

'He's ringing up Medleycott,' said Edward.

Mike came back. We looked at him, not asking.

'Rattled, they were,' said Mike. 'In fact that's the understatement of the year. But it'll be O.K. now. Rescue party on the way shortly.'

'Sorry,' said Edward. His eyes had gone all swollen and shiny. There were bits of straw poking out of his jersey, and dead leaves from last night. His knees sticking out below his grey shorts, were muddy.

'It's not his fault,' I said. 'He couldn't have gone back.'

'I see the problem,' said Mike. 'That's an understatement too. Poor old Edward. Poor old son.'

'Are they angry?' said Edward bleakly.

'I don't think angry's quite the right word,' said Mike. 'It's a bit more complicated than that, what they're feeling.'

I said it, because someone had to. 'Will Betty make him go back?'

There was a pause.

'Look,' said Mike, 'let's not go into that now. I should think there's a chance that things might be sorted out somehow. Why don't we see if Mrs Cheadle could manage some tea?'

Mrs Cheadle is not there, when I go back to that day again. I have no face for her, nor voice, nor form. There is only Mike, saying what he said in the yard, there, with that aeroplane doing its slow creep along the barn roof, and a harrow with one prong missing leaned up against a shed. And a patchy grey and white cat. And then it is getting dark, and we are standing in the lane with Mike and a car is drawing up beside us, with Betty in it, and, heavens! the policeman from Washford.

We were staggered. Policemen meant stealing things, and not doing the blackout properly, and murder. Policemen were serious, not to be trifled with, not to be taken lightly. Stomachs churning, we stood and waited for what might come next. It could have been anything. Perhaps, I thought, and discovered later that Edward thought too, we would have to go to prison.

Betty kissed us, who had stopped kissing us goodnight because we had got too big. And the policeman talked to Mike over our heads and then Betty was saying we must get back. She, too, talked to Mike—a special, restrained kind of talking, like a public telephone conversation.

'Thanks a lot, Mike. I don't know what we'd have done ... Anyway, the less said the better. All right?'

'That's right,' said Mike.

'I'm sorry,' said Edward, to everybody, staring at the ground. And Betty put her hand on his shoulder and said, 'I'll tell you one thing, Samba'll go mad—she's been half out of her mind, everyone gone.'

And I said, 'I'm *not* sorry.'

They all looked at me. The policeman cleared his throat and looked away and then back again.

'I'm not sorry. It's father's fault, not Edward's. He shouldn't have made him go to school when he was miserable. I'm not sorry at all except about Betty and Pam and Susie.'

'Well,' said the policeman, 'there's somebody knows their own mind.' He looked at his watch, and then folded his hands behind his back patiently.

'Trust you,' said Betty. 'Straight to the point and no messing about, that's our Jane. Well, say goodbye to Mike then, you two.'

We said goodbye.

'Come over,' said Betty. 'You've always got a welcome at Medleycott. You know that.'

'Truth to tell,' said Mike, 'I shan't be here much longer.'

'Going to another farm, are you?'

'No,' said Mike. 'As a matter of fact ... Well, the thing is, you see, I've joined up.' He looked at Edward, not Betty, as he said it.

'Well!' said Betty. 'Well, fancy! I am surprised! Well, all the best. All the very best.'

He stood there, Mike, in his earthy corduroys, and his jersey with frayed ends to the sleeves.

'You're going to be a soldier,' said Edward, in a small, stunned voice.

'Yes.'

'But you're a C.O. You can't.'

'That's what I thought,' said Mike. 'But I stopped being quite so sure. People do, you know. It sounds muddled, I know. It is. Things are.'

After a moment Edward said, 'You'd have to kill people.'

'Yes,' said Mike, 'I've thought about that.'

'I thought about running away,' said Edward. 'All night. I know it's not the same,' he added.

'You would have done,' said Mike. 'And it is, in the end. Having to choose. Poor old son. It's no fun, is it?'

They stood there, looking at each other. The policeman had got into the car and started the engine, pointedly.

'Come along,' said Betty. 'You've had half Somerset fussing about you for long enough.'

We got into the car and went away down the lane. When we looked back, at the end, out of the small oval back window, Mike was standing there waving. We went round the corner and he turned back into the farmyard.

We never saw him again. And I do not know what became of him.

'Is that all?' said my husband.

'I suppose it is.'

'He'd be forty-odd now, what's-his-name—Mike.'

'That's right. Funny.'

'He sounds a nice sort of bloke. Let's hope things turned out all right for him.'

'Go slow a minute,' I said.

David's house down at Rodhuish had had a coat of whitewash, and a new gate. He farms somewhere up on the Brendons now, I've been told. A stranger came out and shook a duster, watching us.

'And what did your father have to say about it all?'

Whatever he had to say was not said to us, or not until so long after that the edge had gone out of it and I no longer remember. He went overseas without ever coming down to Medleycott; negotiations crackled over the telephone between him and Betty, that night, while we slept, too exhausted to be curious about what was going on.

'But Edward did go back to school,' said my husband, after a moment. 'You've always said . . .'

'Not then. Not for another year. A reprieve, there was. Betty's doing.'

'Ah. How did he take it?'

'It wasn't quite so bad, I think. He kind of settled down and sweated it out.'

'It was worth it all, then, I suppose,' said my husband.

'Oh, yes.'

'He'd fought back, you mean?'

'Yes. Partly that. I think he felt he'd won something with himself, though, rather than with father, or school, or anything.'

'He wasn't a loser, exactly,' said my husband. 'He doesn't sound that, quite. It's difficult to put your finger on.'

'I know. A victim, do you think?'

'That's a bit glib too,' said my husband. After a moment he asked, 'Did he think of—emulating Mike, as it were—later on?'

'I don't know. If he did, I never heard. He was going to the Royal College of Music. But I've told you that. Could you stop a moment ...'

I just wanted to see the church: Rodhuish church, unadorned and functional as a building in a child's drawing. Whitewashed walls, porch, small tower for the bell. Once, Mr Pitt was the churchwarden and let us ring the bell. It was glorious, a liberation of noise; we filled the landscape with clamour, up to the hills and down to the coast. Now it lay placid in the autumn sunshine, the hills humped around, the deep pink cleft of the lane winding away down to Withycombe. No noise at all except sheep somewhere, and a tractor, a long way off. And rooks, overhead.

I stand looking out of a window, hearing rooks. And

the tick of a clock. A woman with grey hair puts her hand on my shoulder ...

'So you had another year at Medleycott together?' said my husband.

A year, was it? It must have been, I suppose—it seems longer. I only remember it in bits now, snatches.

Samba had puppies, and once her puppies fell into the canal in the iris garden, plopping in one by one as they tried to jump across like Samba did, and we sat in the warm gloom of the airing cupboard, nursing them until they were dry, all wet dog smell and ironed sheets; we had a violent quarrel and I tore Edward's music scores and we didn't speak for a whole day and then made it up and I gave him all my sweet ration; we had mumps; D-day happened.

We went to school in Washford still, but a long, un-smiling young man, exempt from the war because he had something wrong with his chest, pale and thin as string, came to Medleycott on Saturdays to give us extra teaching. Coaching, he called it. We called it lessons. He was somebody's nephew, supplied by Aunt Helen, and he disliked us as much as we disliked him. In mutual bondage we glowered at each other across the playroom table, with furtive glances at the clock, tense for the moment when we could tumble out into the garden and freedom.

Pam got married to one of the soldiers on Treborough Common, in a brief drama of telephone calls to Birming-ham and the Taunton Registry Office. Back from a weekend honeymoon in Devon she was exactly the same, which puzzled us. Marriage, in books, was an ending:

you could not start living happily ever afterwards by being, apparently, the same person that you were before.

People stopped talking about the duration and began to talk about the end of the war. The evacuees down at Rodhuish went home and then, suddenly, came back again because there was new kind of bombing in London now. Flying bombs. David's mum had a new baby and Mrs Curry at the pub died and there was a fire at the Village Hall and the elm at the corner of the lane came down in a storm. Dawn Hosegood started coming up to Medleycott, weekends and holidays, to play with me; Edward made friends with a boy in Roadwater called Tim and vanished with him for long hours into the fields. Betty turned one of the attic rooms into Edward's room and moved his bed up there: neither of us minded. We divided up the books, half each, taking it in turns to choose, so that the Arthur Ransomes got split up between us.

And the second time Edward went away to school is only vaguely with me now. It has no bite to it, like a negative too blurred to print.

'It hasn't been—worrying—coming back?' said my husband.

'Not really. I wanted to, anyway.'

'He must have been about the last lot to go out to Korea?'

'Yes. A year later and he'd have done his National Service on Salisbury Plain, like you.'

I shut the churchyard gate and we got back into the car again.

'You know what,' I said. 'I meant to look in the attic for his violin. Richard could have had that. Damn.'

'Want to go back?'

'No. It doesn't really matter.'

I rolled the window down, to look once more at the church. And hear the rooks.

'Where were you?' said my husband. 'At the time. I don't think you've ever said.'

'Haven't I? Oh, at college. It was my first term.'

A grey-haired woman is sitting behind a desk, in a quiet room where there are many books and a clock ticks. I sit the other side of the desk. She comes out and sits in a chair beside me and talks. She talks and I listen. I have only seen her before across rooms, at the end of tables, speaking from a platform. I see the gold lettering on the backs of books, and hear a quiet clock.

She says, 'My dear, I am so terribly sorry.'

She is, she is. I see her face. She finds it hard to look at me, and I see that she might cry, a grey-haired, public woman.

'This wretched, wretched war,' she says.

And I say nothing. I go to the window and look out, hearing the rooks, and she stands beside me, with her hand on my shoulder. For some reason I cannot think about Edward being dead, but I start to tell her about the running-away time, this strange woman. She listens. I talk and talk.

'Of course you've been back often enough since,' said my husband.

'Oh, yes. Most years, haven't we?'

'He mellowed a bit with age, the old man, one must admit.'

'I suppose so.'

'Did he put the memorial in the church? With all the military stuff?'

'Yes.'

'He had a knack for the inappropriate, your dad.'

'You're telling me.'

'You could always have it taken away now.'

'I don't think I'll bother,' I said. 'It seems neither here nor there, any more. It's a pity about the violin, though. Let's go—we need a hotel before it gets dark.'

We drove fast through the lanes towards the main road.